# THE DAY FORT LARKING FELL

# THE DAY FORT LARKING FELL

▲▲▲▲▲▲▲▲▲▲▲▲▲▲▲▲▲▲

Will Henry

CHILTON BOOK COMPANY

*Philadelphia / New York / London*

Library of Congress Catalog Card Number 68-57511
Designed by Harry Eaby
Manufactured in the United States of America by
Vail-Ballou Press, Inc., Binghamton, N. Y.

# FOREWORD

*Fort Larking does not appear on the maps of western Kansas today. There is a good reason for that. Upon a time, when the region was ateem with buffalo and the feathered red horsemen sat their spotted ponies and watched the white man coming from the East, the fort was known from Leavenworth to Pueblo as the "oasis of the western plains." Its soldiers were not warlike, its officers sought not to rise in rank upon a tide of Indian blood. In especial, its post sutler's store was the magnet of trade for that vast area between the Washita River and the Smoky Hill not served by the older and more famous Bent's Ranch, far westward on the Arkansas. Settler, emigrant, red wanderer and white alike, of every call and color of complexion, knew of Milch's Emporium and all the sundry other civilized aspects of the post made notable by its original and most beloved commander, Major Alexander Kindthorpe. But where Fort Larking flourished once, and good Major Kindthorpe strode in justice among all men, Indian and pale-eyed homesteader favored equally, now whistles only the keening sadness of the wind. Seasons come, seasons go. The snows of many winters have fallen and lain upon the place where pony soldier and painted brave brought arms to bear in the last great combat of the Kansas frontier. Still only the whispering tongues of the buffalo grass remember the dark thing which happened there. The time grows short, if men today would learn the legend, before those rustling leaves of gramma fall forever hushed, and no man knows the sinister truth of The Day Fort Larking Fell.*

THE AUTHOR

# THE DAY FORT LARKING FELL

*To the Waifs and Strays*
*of Every Skin Color*

**1**

THE ANCIENT prairie schooner halted at the crest of the grassy swell. She hung there, topstays groaning, wheel-spokes creaking, ragged canvas whispering in the wind.

The driver, a bearded behemoth in a grizzly-bearskin coat, slacked lines, set brake.

"Ho!" he thundered to his teams. "Yonder flows the Jordan, with beyond the oasis of our salvation. Praise the Lord!"

The mismatched brutes flicked weary ears toward the distant thread of the Arkansas River and the storied cottonwood stockade of Fort Larking, Kansas. Samson, the off-leader, a huge black Spanish jack, walled his eyes wickedly back at the teamster. Wrinkling hairy snout, he made a sound of hideous brass in the temple of the morning's stillness. Delilah, his long-eared mate, joined her hoarse bray to the sacrilege. Preacher Bleek clapped hands to head.

"Blast you!" he roared. "Do you intendfully aim to rouse up from their innocent slumbers within this hallowed ark every last one of these here precious lambs we have carried plumb out of the Land of the Pharaohs?"

The lead team of mules regarded him steadily. The wheel team, a pair of villainous Plains Indian mustangs known as the Kiowa Ladies, twisted ewe-necks and cockle-burred forelocks to study the bearded driver with similar critical calm.

If subdued in any measurable amount, Nehemiah Bleek did not reveal the daunting.

"All right, you precious lambs!" he bellowed over his shoulder. "Every last one of you out and stretch a leg!"

In response to the order, the canvas at the wagon's rear opened to discharge a grinning cargo of dark-skinned Indian children. These were Bleek's foster-chicks, scoured up by him from the battlefields of uncounted cavalry fights, the most recent of which had been a senseless attack by a prowling band of pony soldiers upon a remnant of Stone Calf's Southern Cheyenne camped along a sheltered tributary of the Washita.

To such red waifs Bleek had devoted the unusual store of strength and cunning bestowed upon his great body by a knowing Providence. In the beginning, he had founded a mission school for his Indian strays on Horse Creek beyond Bent's Ranch in the outer Arkansas country. Here he had attempted to instruct the foundling Indian children in ways of survival in an increasingly white frontier world. The work had gone well at first, the older Indians bringing to the gentle giant their weak or wounded little ones to add to the flock of fatherless and motherless youngsters rescued by Preacher himself. The burly white man had honored these trusts for as long as the settlers of the area permitted him to. But, in sad truth, this was only so long as required by those same settlers to learn the nature of Bleek's mission school, which was that the strange man of Horse Creek nourished and cherished the offspring of the so-called "red devils" who raided their towns, scalped their men, ravished their womenfolk, and murdered or carried off their own small children.

2

Then the volunteer cavalry of Colorado Territory had come secretly in the night to burn the mission buildings and take captive the Indian orphans of the Horse Creek school. Bleek had escaped with the children to the Cheyenne camp of Black Kettle on Sand Creek near Fort Lyon. But the Colorado cavalry had followed to destroy that refuge also. Preacher had gathered what he could find of his flock and, hiding them beneath the canvas covering of the Argonaut, his ancient freight wagon, he had fled Colorado as from a pestilence.

In the succeeding months he had tried teaching in other remote and lonely places of the West. Yet always the settlers, the emigrants, the military, the buffalo hunters, the railroad builders—some changing force of the encroaching white world—had come to drive him and his dark brood farther along the road into the wilderness.

Bleek would not quit; he would not abandon his brood.

The need to teach and to protect was there, and he would minister to that need as long as the Lord gave him the breath and the intelligence to do so.

Children came to his various temporary retreats and children went away from them. Some stayed only days, others were still with him from the Horse Creek beginning. Yet others remained a winter, a summer or a fall— long enough to gain some value from the experience— then disappeared into the prairie vastnesses which had produced them. Preacher accepted them all and equally. If there were some poignant thread of first love for the original Horse Creek children, then the Lord would understand and make due allowance. That was what a just God was for.

But if Preacher's faith were a rock, his fortunes stretched thin as spider's silk. In the second year following Sand Creek, after an odyssey of adventures no other

3

white man would—or could—have endured, Bleek found a last home for self and flock with the friendly small Washita band of Stone Calf. Into this happiness had intruded the cruel thrust of the cavalry patrol, forcing Preacher and his orphans of the Argonaut to flee once more along the trackless ruts of the wilderness road.

This time, however, the Horse Creek missionary was determined to find permanent sanctuary for such of his children as he might safely leave behind.

Pausing now upon the final rise before Fort Larking, Preacher knew that the frontier post was the orphaned Indian children's last, best chance for salvation. Yet, as he watched the laughing youngsters mercifully forget the tragedy of yesterday in their rompings about the old wagon, a pang of doubt which he had no words to describe struck deep within him. Nehemiah Bleek was a man as uncomplicated of mind as he was indestructible of bone and sinew. In sheer silent despair he commenced to weep for his dark-skinned little ones.

Six of the youngsters were the survivors of his first school on Horse Creek. The remaining eleven were "wild Cheyenne" from the Washita. These latter were the ones he planned to leave with Major Kindthorpe, ex-agent and friend of the Indian in Colorado Territory, transferred back to Kansas because of his gentle treatment of the "hostiles" in the Arkansas Valley, and said now to be commanding the big post at Fort Larking. His own six children Preacher would keep, traveling on with them to establish one more new school somewhere out toward the sunset. He realized that there must be tearful farewells at the separation. Yet he could neither transport nor feed so many children, and first allegiance lay to his older brood. Moreover, the kindly giant was convinced that good Major Kindthorpe would do all in his power to restore the

4

Washita children to their nearest Cheyenne kinfolk who dwelled along the Smoky Hill River, the next stream north from the Arkansas. All really that remained for Preacher Bleek to do was to reload the youngsters into the Argonaut and roll on down the rise into Fort Larking. Which was exactly why the tears glinted so desperately against his sunburned cheeks, ran so silently to hide beneath the fierce bristle of his red beard.

But a man must see his duty clearly before him and he must never shirk its doing, no matter the deepness of the hurt.

"Ho!" he shouted to the dusky children. "Back into the wagon, you dark-faced cubs of Satan. Praise Jehovah and I'll be shut of the main lot of you come sundown this day!"

## 2

CAPTAIN STRINKER glanced up in annoyance as the trooper entered. "Blemmish, sir," the man said, saluting with a flourish. "Edward A., Corporal of the Guard."

Strinker froze him with a stare. "You fool," he said. "I know who you are. What is it you want, Blemmish?"

"Yes, sir—thank you, sir. There's a jackleg preacher out yonder at the main gate with a wagonload of Injun kids he's gathered up from that there last scrape down on the Washita. Says he wants to leave them here, sir."

"What!" Strinker's voice broke. "On *my* post?"

"Begging your pardon, Captain. This here preacher he don't evidently know it's your post. Thinks Major Kindthorpe is still here. Stanley, sir, that's Sergeant Schmerd, he thinks you'd ought to come out to the gate right quick, sir."

"Blemmish," gritted Strinker. "If you trouble one more time to explain to me who Stanley is, I will put you on hardtack and water for ten days. I know Schmerd, you idiot."

"Yes, sir. But you don't know this here preacher, sir. Leastways that's what Stanley, uh, Schmerd, uh, the sergeant, that's what he said, sir. Begging your pardon, that is."

6

Strinker composed himself. After all, he was a professional leader of men. "At ease, soldier," he waved magnanimously. "We must not lose our heads, eh? Good fellow."

"Oh, thank you, Captain. You're a grand commander, sir."

"One tries, Corporal," admitted the officer. "Now, then, have Schmerd step in here, please. We'll see about all this."

Blemmish saluted and backed out. Strinker's office was at the main gate and it was thus but the work of a moment for the corporal to stride over to Bleek's halted wagon.

"Stanley," he said to the scowling Sergeant Schmerd, "the Captain wants to see you in his office. He's not pleased."

Schmerd shook his burly head. "Shame on you, Edward," he chided. "You just can't run out an order, can you? I told you to have the Captain come out here. I dassn't leave this addlepated preacher and his hatch of prairie quail. They're apt to flush and scatter. They're wild."

"Oh dear," murmured Blemmish. "What will we do, Stanley?"

Bleek, listening to this exchange, wondered what the regular army was coming to. But his time was limited. Stepping down from the wagonbox he called aloud in Cheyenne. Instantly, a dirty-faced little Indian girl put her head out the puckerhole.

"Sunflower," Bleek greeted her, "have you got the dog?"

The tiny girl spoke a stern command in the Indian tongue and a fearsome brute protruded his hairy head beside hers.

"Yes, Preacher," the tot grinned. "Lame Wolf is here."

7

"Good," said Bleek. "Keep a firm-tight hold of his chain."

Schmerd, alarmed, drew back. "What in God's name you got in there?" he demanded. "It sure ain't no ordinary dog."

"It sure ain't," agreed Bleek.

"Cripes!" said Corporal Blemmish. "That there brute is big as a mustang and meaner looking nor a hydrophoby coyote."

"You'd best bear that in mind," nodded Preacher. "Don't try to touch the wagon or them kids whilst I'm gone. The dog's been trained from whelphood to attack white men, especially soldiers. Once sicked, he don't quit. Never."

Before either trooper could react beyond a gulping nod, Bleek took Sergeant Schmerd by the uniform collar and guided him, feet treading air, into Strinker's office.

"It ain't that Stanley, here, don't know his business, Captain," he greeted the startled commandant. "But I'm squoze for time and must be on my way." He set Schmerd back upon his feet, thoughtfully straightening the sergeant's rumpled blue blouse, and giving him an apologetic pat. "Nehemiah Bleek, sir," he continued to Strinker. "Preacher to the red brother of the Arkansas Valley by appointment of the Lord Jesus, I mainly hope. I've come here looking for my friend Major Kindthorpe as used to command at Fort Lyon over to the Colorady Territory. I was told I'd find him in charge here at Fort Larking. Where be he, sir?"

Strinker stared at him unbelievingly. He saw a creature literally furred of face and limb with bright orange-red hair. The fellow was a number of inches over six feet tall and so wide of frame that he went through the door jamb sideways. He was clad in the entire skin of a boar grizzly

8

bear, tanned with the head and claws and tail intact. The effect, taken with a certain unpredictable glitter of the small deep-set eyes and the patently enormous strength of the great body, was such as to unsettle the nerves, to curdle the resolution, to dilute the courage.

Strinker broke his gaze from Bleek with difficulty. When he looked to Sergeant Stanley Schmerd for moral support, that soldier would not meet his glance. Moreover, Schmerd was pale of face and breathing heavily. Perspiration glistened upon his Neanderthal brow. The captain decided to proceed with due and full military caution.

"Major Kindthorpe is no longer at Fort Larking," he explained to Bleek. "He has been relieved of command and ordered east for a board of inquiry on his part in the Sand Creek affair. Something to do with his coddling of the hostiles, I believe. In any event, sir, and until the Major's replacement arrives, I am in temporary command here. All business proper to this post will be directed through me, Captain Julius Caesar Strinker."

It was Bleek's turn to stare. This jackanapes in charge of Kindthorpe's post? A raggletailed Captain taking the place of a true man like the Major? For a penny Bleek would have demoted Strinker on the spot, or disjointed him. But he had his children to think of.

"I reckon," he grudged, "that you will have to do."

He then advised Strinker of the need to leave the Washita children at Fort Larking, assuming that they would be given military escort to their nearest of kin, the Smoky Hill Cheyenne. Here the captain-in-command sniffed disdainfully. His nerve had returned, and the meanness of his small mind with it.

"Sergeant Schmerd," he said. "Place this civilian in arrest."

But Schmerd only paled still more. He did not move. "Beg pardon, Captain," he muttered, "but I'd druther stand to a firing squad. Besides, what's he did that's wrong?"

"Corporal of the Guard!" Strinker was lavender about the lips. Blemmish burst into the room, rifle at the ready. "Arrest this man," raged the officer, pointing at Preacher Bleek. "And Schmerd, consider yourself on report for insubordination!"

Schmerd saluted in acknowledgment of his share of the exchange, but Blemmish did not move to obey Strinker.

"Sir," the corporal of the guard countered, "command me to charge a buffalo herd on foot. Put me in solitary for a hundred days. Shoot me for refusing an order in the field. But please don't ask me to lay hand in arrest to this here peaceful man of God."

Strinker appeared on the verge of a coronary accident but survived the risk. He seemed to realize that he had come upon a decisive moment in his career at command. "Out!" he shouted at both Schmerd and Blemmish. "Schmerd, bring me a cup of coffee. Blemmish, back to your guardpost on the double!"

When the soldiers had gone and before the irate officer might resume with the Horse Creek man, Bleek laid upon him a hand the size of an elk-rump steak. Preacher's voice if gentle had yet within it the warning rumble of heat lightning thunder.

"Captain Strinker, sir," he stated, "I have brung you eleven little kids of the Stone Calf Injun band for succor to this here U.S. of A. army post in peaceful Kansas. I have did it because I have got six orphans of my own to fend for, and because I couldn't think of no one better fitted than the regular cavalry, sir, to see that these innocent red lambs get transported safe to their nearest

10

kinfolk, up on Smoky Hill River. I was hoping to find Major Kindthorpe but I truly ain't the time to go shagging him to Leavenworth, or wherever he be. The Colorado cavalry, they got patrols out looking for me and likewise for any Injun stragglers from that last scrape, orders to shoot to kill."

He paused, sizing up Captain J. C. Strinker.

"You're a cavalryman yourself, sir," he said. "You would know what them horse soldier officers tells their troops; I mean as to taking prisoners—Injun prisoners, that be. So you would understand from that, sir, that me and them little kids of mine—Injun kids—really needs your help desperate bad."

Julius Strinker shook his head, denying the appeal.

"Nonsense, Bleek. I know very well the quality of cavalry officer in frontier service. As a group we are outstandingly humanitarian. Real friends of the red men. Moreover, there is not a cavalryman in U.S. military history guilty of the type of outrage you describe. Now please don't tell me such dedicated men are murdering innocent Indians. That's pure bosh!"

With a stride Bleek pinned him to the office wall.

"I *am* telling you percisely that, and it ain't no bushway, you skinny runt!" He freed Strinker, nodding softly. "Now the question be, Captain, what do you aim to do about seeing that no more such harm don't come to *my* innocent Injuns?"

Strinker, breathing hard, struck a pose of defiance.

"I have here," he said, thumping a sheaf of official papers, "an instruction dated the past week from the Indian Bureau in which I am directed to give shelter to Indian refugees who may come in to this post in result of continuing cavalry field actions. This would include, I assume, the Washita affair."

11

He paused, eying Bleek vengefully.

"As for orphaned children of uncertain origin or degree of governmental responsibility—even, in this case, of some waifs of mixed blood—I have received no specific information. However, I shall warn you what I intend doing with these you have brought in here, and that is to place them in protective custody as wards of the United States Government, and to so treat them until further advised."

"What does that mean?" asked the Horse Creek missionary.

He was watching Captain Strinker with a strange gleam in his small bright eyes. It reminded the officer of the light he had seen in the eyes of an aroused beast, and the chains of caution once more bound his outraged tongue.

"Why," he almost smiled, "that means they will be transported under the very finest of army care to suitable new schools conducted by the Indian Bureau people, whom you know to be on the side of the red man. At these schools, the children will be instructed in every possible way to their best advantage; indeed, sir, to a degree and ultimate totality of success quite beyond your own crude means." He attempted, without notable victory, to enlarge the incipient, sickly smile. "I am sorry, Reverend," he concluded. "But under the terms of the Indian Bureau's instructions, I have no reasonable option save to take custody of your fondlings. This will mean, of course, those you represent as being your own, and those brought from the Washita action, as well."

"Ah," said Preacher softly. "Mine own sparrows, too?"

"You will kindly see Sergeant Schmerd outside." The officer was sniffing again. "He will relieve you of the children. You are free to go as you will."

He arose, extending his hand with a smirk.

12

"*Noblesse oblige,*" he murmured. "The army thanks you—or should, I suppose, Bleek. Not many men would do what you have done."

Nehemiah Bleek eyed him, nodding slowly.

"Not many men would do what I'm going to do now, neither," he said; and, with a tuneful light whistle, he turned and strode forth from the main-gate guard station at Fort Larking, in far Kansas, without another apparent thought for Captain Julius Caesar Strinker, temporarily Commanding.

# 3

WHILE CAPTAIN STRINKER was yet discussing with his aide, Second Lieutenant Cumpston Funder, the mechanics of custody and control of orphaned Cheyenne children, Nehemiah Bleek was swiftly regrouping his threatened force. Preacher was, in fact, leading his small followers out of the parked prairie schooner into the nearby fortress of the post store. "A farsome superior place," as he put it, "for rumping-up to the wall and fighting off the wolves."

Strinker's first hint of this stolen march came blowing across the parade ground with the windy arrival of Henry Milch, the Fort Larking sutler, and a man not without important Washington connections for keeping ambitious captains in line.

"By Heaven, Julius!" Milch raged, kicking in the rickety door to the captain's office. "I may have your commission for this! What have you done to rile that demented Horse Creek preacher? Do you know what he has done, sir? Broken into my store and barricaded himself and all those scabrous Indian brats. And he vows he will not come out until you have given him and all the kids safe conduct away from this post in writing. Now, sir, you start making

14

out that paper this instant, do you hear? The preacher blames you, and so do I. Write—!"

"Nonsense," demurred Strinker. "Come along, sir. I will have this straightened out for you in five minutes. The secret of command, my dear Milch. Something the civilian mind fails continually to comprehend. This Bleek is not really deranged, you know. Merely eccentric."

"The Bleek who threw me out of my own store," said the sutler, "was not *merely* deranged. He was *plenty* deranged!"

"Balderdash!" snorted the captain, but Milch proved the more nearly accurate in his diagnosis.

When the two officers approached briskly across the parade ground, the Colorado missionary called out from inside the store warning them to halt where they were. As Strinker again muttered "Nonsense" and kept coming, Old Bullthrower, Bleek's legendary buffalo gun, bellowed from the building's front window. The big slug struck in front of the officers, sending skyward a plume of dirt not unlike the burst of an artillery shell. Both men stopped in their tracks, clods raining down about them.

"Now, Captain Strinker, sir," called out the forted-up missionary, "less'n you want me to walk my barrage right on up your front buttons, you'd best stand and deliver that there safe conduct paper. Just make it out, and me and my little ones will promise to leave percisely like we come—in peace and Christian confidence, with no harm done—maybe."

The manner in which he added the terminal qualifier cautioned Strinker duly. In his crafty way, the officer turned reasonable and friendly. Indeed, he proved convincing.

Bleek, he argued, must leave the children at the post and himself depart in peace. The Horse Creek preacher

15

was not an educated man and could not expect to bring the actual teaching to his little ones that would be provided by the Indian Bureau. If Preacher would but stop and ponder the problem fairly, he must see that justice to the wild orphans dictated his surrender of them to the government which wanted to help them, and which was prepared to do so. Preacher must also realize that no more such schools as his on Horse Creek would be permitted to flourish. The white settlements, from Montana to Old Mexico, were not going to allow the culturing of young hostiles on their doorsteps. Not when their war-painted parents were burning and pillaging the white community at will. And not, most certainly, while the bulk of the able army troops were spread so thinly on the frontier, as they presently were, to fight the many Indian wars expected by spring. Therefore, Strinker asserted, Bleek must now come out and throw down his gun and deliver his red children to the rightful representative of the rightful authorities—the same being himself, Captain Julius Strinker, U.S. Cavalry, Fort Larking, Kansas.

In the post store, Preacher Bleek stood stricken silent as the stones of ancient Luxor.

Strinker had dealt him a reeling blow.

No man was more acutely aware of his limitations as guard and guardian of his red waifs than Nehemiah Bleek. He was no real teacher. No more than he was a real preacher. He had been a wastrel whiskey-sodden hide hunter and wolf trapper who, bearing daily witness to the tragedy of the lost Indian children, had heard the call. A voice had said to him that he should gather to him and shepherd the small red sheep. He was to teach them the ways of the white man, that they might better survive those ways. He was also to labor to return them, when so taught, to their red people. In this way they might spread

16

his word and help the elders to learn in time that the white man had the power and that the Indian must bow to it, or die. This was the sound of the voice Bleek heard. Glory to the Lord, and amen. The Indian must learn, or he was doomed.

So it was that Nehemiah Bleek now paused in stillness and studied the words of Captain Strinker: if the Indian Bureau truly was prepared to teach the children of the hostile South Plains tribes, its instructors could do the job far better than any score of Preacher Bleeks, or any ten score of such. The imponderable was whether the Indian Bureau people understood how this delicate chore must be undertaken.

Raising his matted beard from his broad chest, Bleek called once more from the front window of the store, seeking to know of the waiting officers if the Bureau schools would be placed in prime hunting country. Would they be built where the grass grew thick and the water was good, and where there was ample wood for warming the cowhide lodges, laying the tipi cookfires? How near—how many pony rides away—would be the buffalo ranges? Would the children be permitted to live with their mothers and fathers, out where the eagle and the hawk swung free? Was it promised they would never be herded and penned upon some barren and sickly-watered reservation? Would they still be free while they were learning the wisdom of the white man's way? How answered Captain Strinker and the U.S. Cavalry to these important things?

The officer at once replied that some of the schools were already constructed. Others would soon be in readiness. But no, none of them was in the buffalo country. All were in, and would be in, areas of settlement and peace. Did not Bleek understand that such location was primary to the object of teaching the Indian children to adjust to civilization?

Did the captain mean, Preacher demanded, frowning, that these schools were, and would be, at such thickly settled places as Lawrence and Topeka and Dodge?

Better than that, even, answered Strinker. He had heard that some of the more fortunate Indian foundlings might go to cities such as St. Louis. There, they would be made wards of the various Christian faiths, of the Protestant and the Catholic, and by these good people taught in the same manner and by the same methods of ciphering as were the white children.

What, as a professed man of God himself, did Preacher Bleek think of that reassuring promise?

Preacher's reply was a deepening of the silence.

So utter was the stillness within and without the post store that the two officers, as well as the off-duty enlisted men who had drifted across the parade ground to join them, later swore they could hear the great indrawing of rageful breath which preceded Preacher's belated roar of anger.

"Curse you!" thundered Bleek at the startled post commandant, "I ain't never going to give up a solitary sparrow of this flock. I would rather see them all dead than a one of them delivered over into such shame. Not to be free, Strinker? You say an Injun child not to be free? Not to have no pony, no bow and arry, no mongrel dog to lie up with of cold nights? 'Fore Christ, Captain, you got ten seconds to get out'n range. And the next shot won't be in the dirt—!"

Strinker did not seem to sense his danger. Funder, also new to the frontier, appeared equally insensate to Bleek's threat.

But Sergeant Stanley Schmerd who, with Corporal

18

Edward Blemmish, was now on the run from the captain's office, came up in time to persuade the inexperienced C.O. and his aide to leave the field. Schmerd had known duty up the Arkansas, was familiar with the reputation of the Horse Creek missionary. "Captain, sir," he panted, "this here man is dangerous. He is nuttier than a peach orchard boar, and will drill you just as quick as he says he will. Folks up the river swear nobody crosses him and comes out first. You may think he's just plain balmy, but he ain't. He's crazy like an Injun. That's why he gets along with the red scuts. C'mon, sir; he's counted to seven!"

From the store building, Strinker could plainly hear the booming knell of Bleek's voice numbering away the seconds.

White-faced, he turned to Funder and gave the order to retreat. The parade ground was cleared of troops, the reserves were sent for, all leaves canceled, a state of siege declared within Fort Larking, Kansas.

Inside the silent store, Preacher's great shoulders sagged. "Children," he said meekly to his huddled brood, "leave us pray." But, even as he said it, the shoulders squared.

He raised his shaggy head, red beard bristling in the musty gloom. "But first, by damn!" he bellowed, "leave us knock the stuffings loose from about sixteen pony soldiers!"

Preacher's immediate problem was the disposition of his forces. First step was to marshal apart the Washita refugees from his own small band. His kids would take orders. They had been in trouble with pony soldiers before. But the survivors of the Stone Calf band were still too frightened, too confused; they would need to be "corraled."

"Red Dust," he said to the oldest of his group, "we got to spy out a hiding place for the wild children, so's we'll be free to fight. You spotted anything suitable?"

The Cheyenne youth nodded. "Over behind the iron fireplace," he said, pointing. "A white man's food cave."

"Ah," said Bleek, "a root cellar. Just right." He took a look out the window. Over toward the barracks, guardhouse, laundry and supply buildings, a great deal of activity was evident. Men were forming up on foot, squad leaders were yelling and waving their arms to impress other squad leaders, nobody seemed to know what anyone was doing, bugles were blowing, dogs were barking—everything was precisely normal for the army.

Preacher nodded. "Here," he said, handing Old Bullthrower to Red Dust. "You keep watch, whiles I hide our poor cousins. Sing out if you see anything suspicious." He patted the long barrel of the heavy Sharps Rifle. "She'll shoot way high at such short range, sights set as they be," he advised. "Hold about the beltbuckle to center their eyeballs."

Red Dust shook his head. He was an intent, sober lad, little given to casual merriment or imprecise exchange.

"I don't wish to kill them, Preacher," he said in Cheyenne. "They have done nothing to me. I will merely throw up a bit of dirt into their eyes, as you did."

It was Bleek's turn to shake his head. But he did so in dismay. He and his dark-skinned charges had an unique arrangement of communication. Preacher spoke English, in order to encourage the Indian children to learn that tongue, while the children spoke in their native language. Why it was they seemed able to understand Preacher perfectly, yet never learn a useful word of English for themselves, was but one of the several mysteries about the big Horse Creek missionary which so baffled and disturbed his white fellows on the frontier. The least charge against him was that he had the Biblical gift of tongues. Others muttered darkly of witchcraft and warlocks and red-bearded overweight werewolves. But Preacher was still able to talk English to wild Indian children, and to be obeyed and answered in guttural Cheyenne, Arapaho, or whatever.

Now, seeing Red Dust's failure to comprehend the seriousness of their situation, he feared there had been some breakdown between them. Before he went to check on the hiding place for the Washita youngsters, he had better hold a council of war with his own educated hatch.

"Huddle up around, you heathen chicks!" he roared to his personal flock. "I'm about to talk a little Injun at you. Ain't no time for trusting white man's words today."

He proceeded in Cheyenne to explain to the children

21

what had been proposed by Captain Strinker for their retention and transportation to unknown schools far to the east where the white man lived in numbers greater than the blades of the buffalo grass. At the words, he saw the fear and the wildness grow in the dark eyes of the small listeners, and he lightened his words at once, yet not untruthfully.

"Wait," he said, holding up his hand and making the Plains Indian sign of confidence and good medicine. "Do you think that Preacher would let them take you away? Do you think your friend of all this time would not know what to do for you? Do not be afraid. We are going to fight, but we are not going to die. We can beat these pony soldiers because the Lord Jesus is on our side. And Maheo, too," he added quickly, including the Cheyenne Allfather as a matter of political expediency. "You need only do what Preacher tells you and, before the moon goes to rest, we will all be away from here and going home to Smoky Hill with the Washita children. Now believe me, my small ones, I will take care of you. But now we must fight. *Nohetto!* Let us get ready."

Since "nohetto" was the Cheyenne term for "that's all," the children all shouted approval of the fighting spirit, and requested Preacher to show them their battle places and also to tell them how they were going to defeat the pony soldiers with only their rabbit bows and arrows, and their prairie dog hole sticks to balance the rifles of the troops.

The spokesman—or rather woman—for this searching remark was Sunflower, the little Arapaho girl. She was the quickest-witted of all the children and, true to her sex, less inclined to show mercy to Preacher's pedestrian mental gaits than her male comrades of the mission

22

school. Now, however, she was not ahead of Bleek. They were in white man's country here at Fort Larking, and Preacher knew his own breed as few of its specimens did. So he only grinned at Sunflower and told her not to think that she was so clever, as Preacher would show them how to fight without guns, and very well, too.

The children took his claim on faith, as they always did, and the huge Horse Creek man told Sunflower to stay with Red Dust and guard the front of the store, while he and the others got the Washita wild children under cover. Then, said Nehemiah Bleek, he would show them how to beat pony soldiers without gunpowder or bullets or killing anyone.

"That's a good thing," said Blackbird, a half Cheyenne, half Negro foundling. "A good fight with no blood around is a fine idea."

"Agreed," said his best friend, Young Buzzard, a bland-witted Kiowa-Comanche youth without a hair on his head. "But I hope Preacher has got some stronger medicine in mind than the Sweet Lord Jesus. The last time we depended on Him, we got—"

"What's this?" demanded Bleek sharply. "The name of our dear Lord spoken in disrespectment?"

"Never!" protested Blackbird. "Unthinkable."

"You dishonor us, Preacher," declared Buzzard sadly. "You know that we pray as you tell us. For Christ's sake!"

"No, no!" cried Preacher in despair. "Not, 'for Christ's sake,' like that. We say, 'in Jesus's name,' or, 'God's Will be did,' but we don't never say what you just said."

"Very well," agreed Buzzard, making the apology sign with owl-eyed earnestness. "Let it be as you say, Preacher; in Jesus's name, by God."

23

"Ahhh," sighed Preacher, "I surrender. Now you two rascals get to the back of the store and look to the bar on that door. Iff'n anybody makes to shake it loose from the outside, set up a holler. Understood?"

"Understood," answered the boys, and set off for the rear of the murky building.

"Now then," said Preacher to his two remaining wards, "come along with me and let's see what kind of a hiding-place scout old Red Dust be. Aha!" He rounded the woodstove and saw a slanted trapdoor, such as was common for root and storm cellars in that country, set snugly against the wall, well camouflaged by boxes and barrels of merchandise. "That boy don't miss a thing. A root cellar, by jings. Just like he said." He went forward quickly, but stopped, the two small Indians crowding behind him. "By damn!" he growled. "Padlocked!"

One of his escorts, a button-eyed disciple no more than five years old, at once stepped forward. "Don't say bad words, Preacher," he piped virtuously. "It isn't nice."

"Oh, God," groaned the missionary. "Be still, Little Chief. Where's a crowbar or axhandle?"

"I can't," said Little Chief.

"You can't what?" yelled Bleek, picking up a five-foot cold steel miner's drill from a nearby counter.

"Can't keep still," said the gopher-cheeked Little Chief. "I've got to make water."

"Sweet Jesus!" said Bleek, sweeping the fat small brave up in one huge hand and bellowing, "Sunflower! Come get your little brother; he's hellbent to wet the floor!"

The Arapaho girl, a cripple whom Bleek had nursed to health, came limping and scuttling as quickly as she might. Taking the youngster by the hand, she appealed to the giant Horse Creek man. "What will I do with him, Preacher? I can't take him outside."

24

"God Amighty, hang him over a pickle barrel!" bellowed Bleek. "I've got a war to fight!"

With the shout, he attacked the lock on the root cellar doors, virtually exploding it with a mighty wrench of the hexagonal steel bar. Whipping up the doors, he started down into the dugout area below, then paused in mid-stepdown, lips rounded, eyes protruding, hands upraised as though blinded by some startling vision beyond earth's ordinary want.

Which, as good Preacher Nehemiah Bleek was given to regard such things, was the case. Or, indeed, the many cases.

Paradise was to hand.

The root cellar was chock-full of bottled-in-bond best bourbon drinking whiskey. There was, glory! glory! enough Old Crow hidden in that dugout hole under store-keeper Milch's Emporium to keep a single man happy from thence to Judgment and half a life thereafter. Praise the Lord; Preacher had stumbled on a smuggled treasure beyond thirstiest, dry-tongued dreams.

"Back, back, little children!" he warned in selfless piety. "Such sight of evil ought never blight innocent eyeballs; nor any other not-so-innocent eyeballs, neither," he added in covetous rumble under breath. "Stand away, dear ones—!"

He reclosed the cellar doors with reverence, already scheming to imagine how much of Milch's illegal whiskey the Argonaut—his wheezing old Santa Fe freighter —might haul away from Fort Larking. And also how such a transfer could be arranged without burning the post to the ground or imperiling his commitment to the Indian children. He had not quite found either answer when Red Dust's excited voice returned him to harsh reality.

"Preacher! Preacher! Come quick, the pony soldiers are

charging at the front door with a naked tree!"

"Jesus save us, a naked *what?!*" shouted Preacher Bleek, and wheeled and sprinted for the forepart of the store.

## 5

Six indians, hostile Cheyenne from Smoky Hill River, rode through the gray-brown silence of the buffalo grass toward Fort Larking. Their leader was Heovese, Yellow Nose. The others were Hoxaven, Cross Feather, Kamax, Stick-of-Wood, Uxtato, Fat, Maxemesevoto, Big Baby, and Hotomemaes, Dog Chips. They were tough, trouble-bound Indians, looking the part. By their accouterments —lance, rifle, bullhide shield, eagle-feather bonnet—they were big for war. Yet Yellow Nose carried no weapons and was armed for peace. On the saddlehorn before him he bore the tribal ceremonial pipe. If his followers were prepared to fight, Yellow Nose seemed ready to pray. To that extent, perhaps, there flickered some faint hope for Fort Larking.

Perhaps, also, the trusty warriors of Yellow Nose were suffering some second thoughts from those noble and fearless ones with which they had set out from the Smoky Hill three pony rides earlier.

Some evidences of better-guessing had obtained.

Indeed, the original delegation had numbered more like sixty, than six, braves. However, with each mile nearer the Kansas post, more men had remembered imperative things they had forgotten to do back home in Colorado—

things which would again be forgotten the moment the conscience-stricken ones had turned tail to minister to ailing squaw, ill friend, aging parent, or whatever. The result was, if not a breakdown of morale, at least a sobering of first estimates as to what the mission might realistically accomplish.

"I don't know," said Stick-of-Wood. "Yellow Nose seems convinced that good Major Kindthorpe will hear our complaints and come and protect us from Yellowhair Custer. See, he still rides out ahead, there, with his pipe and his warbag as sure as a guidestar in the twilight."

"Yes. Well, it's not twilight but sunrise," growled Dog Chips, a surly man who knew a sparrow hawk from a bullbat when the light was early and the wind straightaway. "I remain saying that we should go home and break camp and get away from this country before Yellowhair and his cowardly curs come up to the Smoky Hill. We ought to go north and join our good friend Spotted Wolf in Wyoming."

"Aye," agreed Cross Feather. "That's the true home of our people, anyway. Why did we ever come down to this cursed Arkansas country to live? Our ancestors must have been wrong in their brains."

"Spotted Wolf is a great fighter," offered Big Baby, a gigantic brave with the mind of a four-year-old. "I once saw him take six days to make his medicine, and then he only shot his gun three times and didn't hit anybody. You must be chosen of Maheo to do that."

Fat, a light-skinned man with gray eyes hinting at some former white tipi-sneaker in the family lodge, and who, perhaps because of the alien blood, had little patience with Big Baby's limited intellect, snorted disdainfully. "Ha! Speaking of the choices of Maheo, He should have selected a bigger brain for stuffing in that bulging head of yours. I think if you shake that head very hard, you will hear the rattle of the brain. It is like a dried bean in a buffalo skull. Ho, ho, ho!"

The others permitted Fat to laugh alone. It was not good Indian behavior to make fun of the demented or the weak of mind. But Big Baby was not so critical.

"Thank you, friend Fat," he said. "I love to hear you laugh. It sounds like Brother Coyote with his tongue caught in a rabbit snare."

"Enough! Enough!" cried Yellow Nose, turning in his saddle. "Come up here, all of you, and listen with me. I thought I heard something in the morning air."

The five braves rode up quickly. At once, the only sounds were the snuffling of the ponies, the soft pass of the wind.

"What was it?" asked Cross Feather.

"Gunfire, I think," answered the leader. "There, you hear that?"

"*Iho!*" breathed Dog Chips. "Pony soldier rifles!"

"Aye," said Stick-of-Wood. "From down along the river by the fort. Maybe some others of our people have beaten us to come and talk with good Major Kindthorpe."

"With *guns?*" demanded Fat, scowling disgustedly. "Sometimes, Kamax, I think you are no smarter than Big Baby."

"But still brighter than you, eh, Uxtato?" said Stick-of-Wood, crowding his pony into that of the light-skinned brave.

"Here, stop that bickering!" ordered Yellow Nose. "Remember, we're on this journey to ask help of the Kansas soldiers against Custer and the others in Colorado."

"They won't give us any help, if that is Indians they are firing at," said Cross Feather.

"That is so," declared the dark-faced Dog Chips. "I am ready to fight the soldiers, if we find they are shooting at Indians down there."

"Wait! Listen!" cried Yellow Nose, holding up a skinny red arm. "That's no Indian gun."

The Cheyenne leaned forward, ears to the rustle of the prairie breeze. The distant sound of the alien rifle boomed heavily as cannonfire, and Dog Chips brightened visibly.

"By Maheo's navel-fuzz!" he shouted. "That's a buffalo hunter's big rifle. The soldiers are shooting at their own hunters. The white men are killing each other, not Indians. How wonderful! Let's go and watch."

"By all means," agreed Cross Feather, turning his pony.

"Wait!" cried skinny Yellow Nose. "I am the leader; I ride first."

But his faithful followers were already spurring their shaggy mustangs over the waving buffalo grass toward Fort Larking, and it was all that Yellow Nose's spotted pony could do to keep up with the band, let alone regain the lead.

The wiry pipe-bearer of the Smoky Hill "peace mission" stood in the stirrups of his stolen cavalry saddle, lean face upraised to the morning sky, dark arm and clenched fist shaking under the nose of Maheo.

"Indians!" shouted the man of moderation. "Sometimes I wish you had covered me with white skin, you no-good God! You whelped us all with crazy heads. It's no wonder the white man wins all the time!"

PREACHER BLEEK, staring from the barricaded front window of Henry Milch's post store, saw that the "naked tree" of Red Dust's alarmed warning was indeed a battering ram. It was, in exact fact, a telegraph pole requisitioned from the supply depot behind the stables. Its iron climbing angles made ideal hand-holds, and by these grips the troopers, six to a side, were presently rushing the barred front door of Milch's Emporium. With no time for higher strategies, Preacher merely bawled to the boys on the rear door to swing wide that exit when he, Preacher, also opened the front door. The children believed their burly guardian had lost his mind powers but, as he had in faith understood that they would, they obeyed him blindly. Thus, the battering ram soldiers swept in the front and right on out the back of the store without their weapon striking any object, or any Indian child, and indeed encountering no solid resistance of any nature until thirty paces into the rear yard of the store. There, they brought up ringingly against the understructure of the post water tower, collapsing it with their ram and bringing down upon themselves every fit drinking drop inside the compound, as well as the slimy staves, circling them all corsetwise, of the tank itself.

If not a definitive victory, the swift action was, at its smallest power, an opening portent of tactics to come.

And it gave Preacher a little time to arrange his defenses; to get the wild Cheyenne children hidden behind a counter of camouflaging drygoods; to issue detailed instructions to his combat troops on various effective, if militarily humane, methods of confounding the enemy.

When the enraged Captain Strinker shortly reorganized his assault forces and ordered the renewal of the attack, it was not en masse but along guerrilla lines—each trooper directed to rush and get into the store the best way that he himself might devise. Once inside, he was to first admit his fellow troopers, then turn to the work of subduing Bleek. The children, actually, were ignored in the combat orders—a most grievous error as events quickly disclosed.

The first soldier to be struck with military inspiration decided that he saw an opportunity for promotion to corporal by hoisting himself to a high side window of the store and striking the enemy on the flank. Instead, when he wormed through the unguarded port, he found it not unguarded but rather armed with a coal chute. This chute had been so placed by Preacher and his people that its burnished slide led the intruder directly into an opened barrel of blackstrap molasses. When fighting his gluey way free of this baptism, he was given another via a slit featherbed mattress brought down over his dripping head by Buzzard, Blackbird, and the sixth of Bleek's dark brood, a little Mexican-Apache halfblood named Santiago.

"*Hola!*" shouted the latter, a lad of constant optimism, and gave the blinded soldier a shove toward Preacher who, gathering him in, rushed him out the front door onto the parade ground. Here his appearance, momentarily suggesting that he had been tarred and feathered, brought some panic to the remaining troops. This disarray was not improved when a second trooper, having followed the first through the same side window, burst from the store in scarcely better plight. This one had been received down the chute into the slit mattress itself, the mattress then closed about him and tied-off at his waist by Preacher's great strength. But, too, the Horse Creek missionary had lighted the feathers of the bedtick with a bit of coal oil and a brand from the stove. The second cavalryman galloped out of the emporium bawling in what he was convinced were his death throes, and which convinced his fellow troopers that he was being incinerated alive and before their very eyes. Nor was this even the beginning of the end. Even as the first two men blundered about the parade ground yowling for help, three more who had gained entrance to the store through a back window came stumbling out pawing at a mixture of blackstrap and white sackflour with which Preacher and his wards had anointed them.

Strinker, of course, turned livid.

This was worse than anarchy—it was insanity. He forthwith called up the artillery, a two-gun battery of four-pound mountain howitzers. Wheeling these into position, he threatened to blow Bleek and his Indian children into a sooner Kingdom Come than they had bargained for, unless Preacher flew the white flag at once from the store's front window.

Since Bleek's answer was a wordless bellow of defiance, and since no pale guidon fluttered from the shattered glass of Fort Milch, the captain raised his sword to order the bombardment begun.

At this point Sergeant Schmerd respectfully begged to suggest that some more certain form of pressure be brought to bear on Bleek, since no one had been able to find the shot for the cannon and they were presently loaded with nothing more frightening than black powder and wiping rags.

On the point of weeping, Strinker was advised by his aide, Lieutenant Funder, that, even without shot, the cannon might be effective. How would Bleek know they were not loaded? The artillery in its historic use in Indian warfare had been psychological anyway. No known document or record existed to prove that a solitary red man had even been so much as singed by cannonfire, yet it was known that the red heart turned to white water when the flames belched and the wheels bucked to the elegant bellow of the howitzers.

The truth was that Cumpston Funder, a man far too long trod upon by more hirsute rankers, had tasted blood. Strinker, having no better plan, unleashed the bespectacled lieutenant with orders to reduce the rebel fortress within the hour, or face the future as the only thirty-year-in-grade shavetail in the history of the U.S. Cavalry.

As for Captain Strinker himself, he was much too distraught to be of further help. Sensibly, he ordered himself out of service and escorted to the post kitchen. Here, he reasoned, a quart or so of Mrs. Mehaffey's hot and powerful black coffee might restore a modicum of the resolute heroism traditional with the Strinker military men under fire.

As for Funder, with the hapless C.O. out of the way, that brave youth turned to the serious business of war, shrill voice and pallid form inspiring the indifferent men to firm ranks and return to the assault.

The advance this time was made under a progressive smoke screen, a rolling barrage, as it were, of howitzer grease-rag fire. Behind the screen, the troopers were able to invest the store and come to grips with Preacher Bleek.

Here, precisely, lay the trouble.

With a joyous shout to the Lord to labor on his side, Preacher threw off the mere seven or eight soldiers who first had seized him, and lay-to, as he put it, "to tromple down the vintage where the grapes of wrath was stirred."

The big-eyed wild children of the Washita crouched behind their counter refuge and watched in awe. They had seen the pony soldiers at war within the present moon. Some of them were old enough to remember Mad Dog Chivington's slash-in-the-night at Sand Creek. But none of them had witnessed, nor dreamed in brightest nightmare to witness, such havoc as Nehemiah Bleek now wrought among the invading ranks of the pony soldiers.

"Mine eyeballs have see'd the Glory!" thundered Preacher, and closed with the enemy.

The astonished troopers whom he had just brushed back with windmill sweeps of his great post-oak arms had no time to recover. Bleek took up the front twain of them by their belt buckles and knocked their foreheads together so hard that the nose of one caught in the teeth of the other and they fell to the floor not only unconscious but bound together and gagged. Next, he seized up a single trooper, took him by the ankles, giant-swung him as a horizontal pinwheel, mowed down with this human scythe the remaining half-dozen of the original attackers. By this time, the main column was coming up fast through the smoke to encircle Preacher with carbines at the ready, forcing more sophisticated tactics. Preacher was ready.

With a single bound, he cleared the top of the nearest counter, that of the Hardware & Horsefeed section. Putting his thick shoulder to the counter, he moved the entire barricade free of its nailed moorings in the emporium's floor and, pushing it ahead of him like a railroad grader, caught up some fifteen to twenty troopers and rushed them backward into the opposite wall where, pinned between the mobile counter and the unyielding butt-sawn Arkansas cottonwood wall, they were crushed breathless.

Pulling the counter away from them, Preacher permitted the victims to slide down the wall to sitting postures in a neat line on the floor, paralyzed. To the Horse Creek children who by now had fallen in behind their grizzly-coated chaperone, Bleek gave greeting and instruction.

"Here," he said, picking up a wooden crate marked Bung Starters and breaking it open by smashing it on the counter of Hardware & Horsefeed. "Each take one of these wood beer-barrel tomahawks and quieten-down this row of Hittites. Yonder comes the cavalry of Nebuchadnezzar from out'n the Plains of Shinar. Ho! ye Babylonian hosts! Come and git it!"

Now Preacher reached down from the nearby wall two blacksnake mule whips of twelve-foot lash and advanced to lay among the closing troops with rawhide tongue, a curling thong in either hand, with mule skinner's oath to match.

Red Dust marshaled the staring Horse Creek children to obey Preacher's order, saying, "Come on, don't worry about Preacher; pray for those poor pony soldiers. Meanwhile, we have our own work to do with these several sitting on the floor."

What the work was, was that the Indian children went down the line of stupefied troopers and, politely removing the campaign hat of each, struck the warrior over the skull with the rawhide-bound wooden head of the bung-starter mallet each had taken up from the crate sundered by Preacher. As each child would smite the soldier of his choice, he would murmur politely in Cheyenne, "*nononaoan,* excuse me, please," and carefully replace the hat upon the soldier's head as the latter's eyes rolled upward and set hard while his fluid body slumped on down the wall to spread, loose-jointed, upon the floor.

Preacher Bleek had suffered no disrespectful nor ill-mannered child in his school.

As this courteous head knocking proceeded, Preacher himself surged into smoke-shrouded advance of Funder's expeditionary force roaring to shame the Bull of Bashan.

Beady blue eyes shining purely, he kept yelling his version of the Battle Hymn—"He is swiping at the Wickud with His turrible Swiss s'ord!"—and cutting at the unfortunate troopers something sinful with the leather blades of his mule skinners' twin stilettos. The encircling force fell away, and back. Even a jackass got the point of a blacksnake whip flayed into him by an expert. Retreat neared rout.

Just in battle's time, Funder was able to get up to the deteriorating front a suicide squad of six bayonetmen.

But Preacher had his way with these heroes, also.

Sweeping up one of them by the feet with the snaring loop of the skinner's whip, he would drag the lad to him, disarm him of bayonetted carbine, jam the weapon by its razored steel into the rough log wall, and hoist upon the walnut-butted peg thus formed, the uniform collar of the luckless pony soldier, same soldier still inside the collar. So panther-quick was the huge Horse Creeker, and so high did he string up the bayonet squad by its collective collars, that Funder had no sooner committed the unit to the breech than it was kicking its heels against the cotton-wood logs and squalling for mercy in surrender.

The battle teetered now in the balance.

But Preacher's fortunes of war were changing even as the issue labored in doubt.

A bag of white flour, swung from a rope dabbed over a

roof joist by the inventive Red Dust, went awry in its aim. Instead of whistling past Preacher in its descending arc, to burst in the faces of his advancing enemies, the arc of the bag sagged a bit, while, for his part, Preacher turned around at just the wrong time.

Whhaapppp-ploooshh!

The bag took the red-bearded giant square across his broad cheekbone. It struck exactly amid his blinking blue eyes. It flew apart to explode in Preacher's face, blinding him.

What sixty troopers had not done, Red Dust brought to pass, alone.

Preacher was groping. He could not see.

And, with a mighty cheer, the pony soldiers charged.

▲▲▲▲▲▲▲▲▲▲▲▲ **7**

SEEING THEIR Palladin stricken, the Horse Creek children rallied desperately to his aid.

For an incredible moment in cavalry and Indian warfare it seemed as if the dark tides of the Washita and Sand Creek might be reversed in the bloodless but bone-shattering Battle of Milch's Store. Certainly young Red Dust and the others intended harm to those pony soldiers. As certainly, they wreaked upon Funder's men a worthy vengeance. The coups, counted with bung-starter mallet by Blackbird, Buzzard, Santiago, and the nephew of the mighty Roman Nose upon toe, shin, pate, and clutching finger of the troopers closing about Bleek, were of great courage. Yet Preacher was still blind and, like Samson in the temple, must go down at last.

The troopers came upon him with manacles of mule harness, log chain, and trace tug to bind him as he fell beneath their rain of vile rifle-butt and boot blows. The six Horse Creek children were sacked like coyote cubs in empty flour bags thrown over the entire child and draw-stringed at ankle by makeshift lariats of picket rope. The helpless Washita waifs were herded together and driven ahead of the fighting missionary and his flour-bagged flock out of the splintered store into the smoke-hazed daylight of the parade ground.

There Lieutenant Cumpston Funder, feeling the primeval power of command rising within him higher still, flung up his fringed gauntlet. It was his intent to voice the order which would dispatch the prisoners of war to the guardhouse. He himself would lead the procession, and he would direct it past the mess hall where the effete Captain Strinker might see what a real soldier did with derelict leadership.

But another commander had come on the field.

He was not trained in the tactics of von Clausewitz, nor of Sherman, but was a cavalryman of nature. Also, he was a creature of the heart. And it made his heart bad to see the children dragged in sacks by their heels, and the other refugee youngsters herded like animals, and, *ih-hi!* wasn't that Preacher Bleek there in those mule halters and blinders and all bound about with wagon chains? By Maheo, what sort of pony soldier trick was this? What did that silly-looking young one-bar chief think he was doing to the children of Preacher, and of the Cheyenne?

*"Wagh!"* shouted Yellow Nose, in the universal courage-word of the high Plains tribes. Then, as the startled lieutenant and his troopers whirled about, he concluded in the halting fractured tongue of the white brother. "What hell you do him Preacher Bleek, him Cheyenne Injun kid?"

Funder was for the instant held dumb.

Where the devil had those six mean-eyed hostiles materialized from? The clear blue? But then it came to the temporary C.O. of Fort Larking, Kansas, that in the excitement of subduing Bleek and the Horse Creek brats, the main gate had been left untended for the better part of half an hour. The hard-staring guests had simply walked their ponies in out of the open prairie and up

40

through the deep dust of the parade ground unseen in the turmoil of the siege.

All right, then, but what of this challenge to Cumpston Funder? Had his ears betrayed him, or had that dwarfish brave in the oversize, groundsweeping feather bonnet just demanded of him to know what the hell he thought he was doing with the Reverend Nehemiah Bleek and the Indian children of his shepherdhood? The lieutenant, feeling the eyes of his silent men upon him, knew action must ensue. He did not need Sergeant Schmerd's low-voiced reminder that the troops were growing smirkful, and he stomped his foot petulantly, three times.

"Be still, Schmerd!" he scolded. "You're not dealing with Captain Strinker here."

"Yes, sir," saluted Schmerd. "But that there little Injun is still putting the snake-eye on you, sir, and something has got to be did, or you will lose face."

Funder knew a moment of military panic. The five Indians behind the tiny leader were crowding their stunted mustangs toward him and the troops. The steel clinks of their rifle hammers being put upon the cock could be heard distinctly. "Schmerd!" he whispered from the side of his mouth. "What is generally done in a situation such as this?"

"You need an interpreter, sir, to talk to them."

"Do we have one on the post?"

"Yes, sir. Bleek yonder. He can jabber their tongue better than they can."

"Get him up here and tell him to begin at once an exchange with these savages. We must not have any trouble here, my first chance in command."

"Oh?" said the sergeant. "I didn't know you was in command, sir. I thought the Captain, he just went to get hisself a cup of coffee."

"You insolent dog!" snapped Funder. "Get that jackleg preacher up here this instant!"

Schmerd ordered Bleek dragged forward and then told the Horse Creek man what was expected of him. Bleek nodded and began a guttural dialogue with the Indians. Soon he turned to Lieutenant Funder, no hint of animosity in his sober face and soft voice.

"They come here to talk with Major Kindthorpe, same as me," he told the young officer. "They're looking for protection from them Colorado troops, same as we be."

"Well, well, what of it, man? You know Captain Strinker's answer on that. Tell them to be off, and no tricks."

Bleek shook his head, advising the lieutenant that the hostiles were all well-known men among the Smoky Hill band of hostile Cheyenne. The leader, Yellow Nose, was not to be misjudged because of his small stature. He was an orphaned Ute, one of Bleek's earliest students, and had been adopted into the Cheyenne tribe as the son of old Spotted Wolf and his wife Wind Woman. No meaner blood existed in the fighting Cheyenne people, and Yellow Nose had been reared to avoid the white man when he could, kill him when he could not ride around him. Lieutenant Funder would be well advised to listen closely to what the chief was saying.

Funder stomped his foot again and said that this was precisely what he wanted to know—what the chief was saying. Would Bleek be so good as to tell him, please?

Well, Preacher nodded, yes he would.

The lieutenant wasn't going to like it, however. What the runted Cheyenne was demanding was that he, Funder, turn loose Bleek and all the Indian children, apologize to each for the bad treatment, permit them to leave the post with the Cheyenne, and no pursuit.

42

"Insane!" cried Funder. "Utterly absurd!"

"Yes, sir," agreed Bleek. "That's your Injuns for you every time, Lieutenant. What do you want me to tell them?"

"Tell them to get out of here this instant, or—no, wait —what is the option? The rest of the threat?"

Preacher shrugged, palmed his huge hands. "Yeller Nose, he says iff'n you don't do what he says, he'll attack the fort."

"*What?* With five men!?"

"Not hardly, sir; he ain't no fool."

"Well, I should think not!"

"No sir, he aims to do it all by hisself."

Funder recoiled. Was this hairy lout making fun of him? Attempting to belittle him in front of his men? Incredible!

"You, sir," he charged Bleek, "are daft! I will not suspect you of greater accomplishment, but beware, I warn you!"

"I thank you, Lieutenant," said Preacher soberly. "What you want I should tell this here Injun, sir? War or peace?"

Strinker's skinny aide drew himself erect. He had heard the sniggering of the troops at Bleek's naiveté, and knew he faced one of those historic moments of command-decision which separated combat officers from barracks brigadiers or schoolbook soldiers. Upon his next action might depend a future to rival Custer's, Crook's, or Fighting Phil Sheridan's. Cumpston Funder was ready.

"Tell him," he squeaked loftily, "to go to hell."

Bleek knuckled a furry eyebrow, turned to the waiting Cheyenne horsemen. When he had spoken briefly to them, the five warriors behind Yellow Nose turned their ponies and departed the post. A short way off on a prairie elevation where a spring-branch bubbled up and where three cottonwoods stood sentinel, they dismounted and made camp. As soon as they were out of the gate, their wizened leader got down off his mount and stalked to a position directly in front of the sutler's store. There, he drew a circle in the dust in the exact middle of the company street. In the center of this he kindled a small blaze, tossed upon it some blue powder from his medicine bag. Bright orange smokepuffs burst upward in acrid clouds. Peering through the looping curls of this murk, the curious troops saw Yellow Nose take from the same bag an ancient flute of eaglebone. Upon this eerie-noted pipe he began to play an Indian cadence which, despite the mid-morning warmth, caused gooseflesh to flower along the white spines of his audience. At the same time he commenced to gyrate in slow, halting stomps about the fire, and to intone a singsong chant in his mother tongue.

"What is the rascal up to now?" Funder demanded of the interested Bleek. "Some display of fawning appeasement, I should suppose. A man stands up to them and they run like yapping mongrels. Hmmmpff! Well, sir, you may tell him for me that I shall be unmoved by his pleas. When he is through with his foolishness, Bleek, I want you to instruct him to pick up his childish trash and go home and behave himself. Be quick about it, man. I've got to get you and these red whelps of yours into protective custody."

"Yes, sir," said Bleek. "Howsomever, there's one little question, Lieutenant—Yeller Nose, he ain't begging no mercy, sir; he's declaring war."

"*What!*" fumed Funder. "War? On whom? What?"

"On this here whole entire fort, Lieutenant, just like he said he would."

"See here, Bleek, don't try my patience. I've warned you once. You've seen me aroused."

"Oh, yes sir," saluted the Horse Creek man. "And ter-

44

rible impressive you was, too, sir. But no matter, sir, old Yeller Nose he's a'going to charge you when he's done making his medicine."

"Why, that's preposterous, man! He hasn't even a weapon."

"That's the whole point, Lieutenant; he ain't. So you will have to shoot him down, unarmed, and there you'll have your dead Cheyenne chief who come to see you in peace and, well, Lord knows where it all might end, sir. You know, I mean for the futures of them as was in command here at Fort Larking the day Yeller Nose was kilt in cold blood by orders of Lieutenant Funder, or whosomever, sir. A entire garrison of U.S. of A. cavalry soldiers firing on one poor little old puny runt of a Smoky Hill Cheyenne Injun which was only trying to—"

"Stop, stop!" cried Funder, throwing both hands skyward in surrender. "You miserable blackguard, you!"

"Miserable as may be, sir," nodded Bleek. "But powerful accurate."

"Yes, yes," grimaced the young officer. "Good Lord, Bleek, you're a monster. You've the intellect of a pirate."

"It ain't only me, sir; all these here honest young soldiers will have to say what they saw, sir; what orders they was give, and by what officer. Now, iff'n I was—"

"Be still this instant, sir!" commanded Funder, stamping his foot. "You are not me and I shall issue the orders here." He paused, glaring helplessly at Preacher. "Sergeant Schmerd!" he shouted. "Over here at once, if you please!"

When Schmerd had shuffled up, Funder gave him instructions to rope off an area in front of the store, and around Yellow Nose's ceremonial circle, and to see that no soldier violated that space, or so much as put hand or tongue to its occupant.

"Let the fool have his dance," he concluded. "In a

command situation of this nature the superior white intellect must be demonstrated. Remember, absolutely no harm must come to this Indian. Do you understand, soldier?"

Schmerd saluted and said that he did. But when Funder wheeled about to see to the disposition of his escort troops for the prisoners' march to the guardhouse, the simian-eyed sergeant sidled up to Bleek quickly.

"Say, Reverend," he asked, "how long's this heathen red ape apt to go on thisaway? And what's he working hisself up to, anyhow? Starting it to come on to rain, or bringing back the buffalo, or what?"

Preacher raised his chained arms, and patted the anthropoidal trooper comfortingly on the shoulders.

"Be of good heart, my child," he counseled. "He may dance for ten minutes, or eight hours, or all night, but when he is ready he is going to attack the U.S. Cavalry at Fort Larking."

"Preacher," said Schmerd, backing away, "you're cracked!"

Bleek nodded, and turned to go as he felt the prod of a trooper's bayonetted rifle take him in the haunch.

"So is that little Injun chief dancing yonder, Stanley," he said to the scowling Schmerd. "Be constant keerful of him, you hear? Don't dast to turn your quarters to him."

"Be still!" yelled Second Lieutenant Cumpston Funder, flourishing his saber from column-head. "Prisoners of war, forward marchhh— Ho!"

# 8

KATHLEEN MEHAFFEY had never seen the day against which she could not prevail. Wee Katie, as her "so'jer boys" of the Fort Larking garrison called her, was, to tweak the Celtic phrase, "a broth of a lass." Weighing a lissome fourteen-stone-and-four, standing five-feet-fair in her U.S. Infantry brogans, light as a thistle upon her feet, quick as a she-bear and as potent, with either chubby paw, of an Irish wit to shackle Beelzebub or lead astray a leprechaun, she was a match for any man; or so she firmly believed.

And, as to that, what Wee Katie believed, Wee Katie achieved—or speared, or snared, or convinced, or contused, or destroyed altogether—and in the end, whichever way, made good Wee Katie's faith in Wee Katie.

In present pause she was ministering to the vapors of Captain Strinker, plying the distraught C.O. with bituminous coffee and Hibernian wile to the military point where he might once more resume composure and command.

"Shure now, Captain darlin'," she cooed, " 'tis scarce a derrylikshun of jooty to layve the smoking-out of a haythen scut of a Protestant, ah, of a poor misguided haythen praycher, to the loikes of Lieutenant Funder."

She flowed around the table, poured more coffee into the despondent officer's cup, sympathies veering swiftly as the dart of a weasel's eye. "On the other hand, me boy, them little childrun is another matter, bejabbers. If so much as an oyelash of thim blissed redskin lambs be harmed, I'll flay that Funder aloive!"

She subsided like a beached whale athwart the chair opposite Strinker. An arch smile lifted the carroty brows. The fey elfin wink of Erin twitched the blue-green eye. "Ah, now, Captain dearie," she chirruped, "whut's he loik, this infidel Praycher of the Plains? Shure and I've hurd a few tayles that wud tingle the ears of enny daycent gurl."

Strinker colored in protest. "I know absolutely nothing of the rascal, Mrs. Mehaffey," he stammered. "Except that Bleek is a mental case and a menace to frontier society. I intend to hold him on the post until advised of his disposition, and that of his foundling brats, by higher authority."

"Yez plan to put the Praycher in the guardhouse, thin?"

"Under twenty-four-hour guard, madam—yes indeed."

"And the little wans? Whut of thim, the innocent dears?"

"I had intended asking you to care for them, Mrs. Mehaffey. Would you be so kind?"

"Faith and of carse. Thank yez, sor. The poor things will be near desprit for a daycent meal and a clayne place to slape, to be shure. I'd bist get riddy for thim, lah!"

Strinker, thinking to hear the unwelcomely familiar tread of marching feet, glanced out the steamy window. "Too late, madam," he intoned glumly. "The little devils are already here. That fool, Funder; he has brought them by this way while conducting Bleek to the post prison under guard."

"Ah! the Praycher, yez say?" The dainty avalanche spilled around the table to peer, with Strinker, through the clouded pane. "Here, Captain darlin', let's have a sharpher peek at yur monster, sor. Swate Jayzus—!"

Coming to a deep-gasped halt, pug nose flat to the dank pane, Kathleen Mehaffey stared, blindstruck, out the window of the post kitchen. Of a wondrous-sudden her wild Irish heart was ablaze with a yearning more feral than that of the legendary cats of Kilkenny.

"Yez black-souled Hessian!" she cried out against the startled Strinker. "Be that the haythen praycher yez've bin telling me yur dirty foul-tongued lies about, yez treacherous jack-booted divil!?"

Strinker staggered back from the table, fending off her fury with his chair.

"Down! Down! Madam!" he shouted. "Control yourself. What in heaven's name has come over you? Do you want me to call the post surgeon? Quick! Are you in pain?"

Wee Katie fell away from him, half aswoon. Her eyes re-opened in the moment to flash the fires of a thousand burning prairie nights. Her vast bosom heaved and thrust and billowed on as the seas of the buffalo grass before the coming storm. Her voice held the clarion joy of the barren cow elk, the shrill gladness of the blighted buffalo heifer.

"In pain, yez blithering jacksnipe!" she bellowed at Strinker. " 'Tis luv I'm after being in, Captain darlin'!"

# 9

THERE WAS a scene of some petulance between Captain Strinker and his aide outside the post kitchen. It seemed that Strinker suspected Funder of ambitions to command which the captain reserved to himself. The lieutenant was forthwith instructed to take duty in charge of the post prison guard to be set up over Preacher Bleek.

Further changes in arrangements were necessitated when the attempt was made to separate the good preacher from his six lambs. It was one thing to herd the frightened Washita children into the company kitchen, quite another to convince Red Dust and his blooded fellow resistance fighters of the Battle of Milch's Store that they should abandon Preacher to the unknown mercies of the pony soldier guards.

The Horse Creek children, although still sacked like prairie-trapped coyote whelps, began to yip and kick and ki-yi with such effect that Strinker feared a return of their Smoky Hill relatives from the peaceful cottonwood camp outside the stockade. Moreover, there was already the Indian matter of Yellow Nose doing his medicine dance in front of the post store with which to contend. Strinker, informed now of this development by Funder, nearly had another relapse. Managing to control his rebellious nerves, he ordered the Horse Creek kids to be taken along to the guardhouse and put into the spare cell next to Preacher's. In this way, at very least, some peace would be established during which Strinker and Funder might council to see how deeply-in they had gotten themselves by crossing the hairy giant from the Arkansas.

The matter of whether to put the report of the affair on the telegraph wires for area command at Fort Leavenworth, or whether to clamp down a rigid security on and about Fort Larking until some more favorable control of the outbreak had been established—hopefully through some reasonable treaty with Preacher and his tribe—was a question of the most serious nature. Strinker and Funder agreed on this quickly, and leaving the Cheyenne children with the bosomy Mrs. Mehaffey, marched off with Bleek and his mixed-blood brood to the post guardhouse. Here the jailings were made with no further skirmishes or troop casualties.

The two officers then conferred the afternoon away.

The situation was most iffy. Fort Larking's normal garrison was of some 150 men, plus commissioned and noncommissioned staffers to the regular complement. But presently an escort had been detailed to some junketing Congressmen from the East, another detail of men was cutting hay far off to the south, still another group getting in timber and firewood for the winter in an even more remote location. Runners were of course dispatched to bring these reinforcements home at fastest march. But with the best of luck the lawmakers' escort would be gone a week, while the hay and wood details would require forty-eight hours to reach the post. Meanwhile, should word leak out of the troops wounded by Bleek in Milch's store, of the property damage to the sutler's goods and building, and of the inestimable weakening of morale at Larking, where that spirit had already slumped to half-mast with the departure of popular Major Kindthorpe under official cloud, the odds on Strinker ever making field grade, or Funder seeing a first lieutenancy, would be about like those of the Alamo against Santa Anna. It would seem that Strinker and Funder, with no other commissioned officers to support them, and only the Stygian-witted Schmerd and Blemmish for noncoms, with something like one full troop of raw cavalry recruits and three squads of infantry work troops on roster for the day, had their work well laid out before them.

"Cumpston," said the captain, summing up, "this is our fight and we must finish it."

"Agreed, sir!" piped the lieutenant, saluting smartly.

Then the two of them sagged in their chairs and sat staring at one another, knowing the full enormacy of the decision just taken. They were still in this gray-faced posture of shock when Sergeant Schmerd entered the office.

"Begging your pardon, sir," he said. "But it's sundown and we're taking in the flag."

"Very well, Stanley," sighed Strinker. "Lieutenant Funder and I shall be right out. What's the situation at the store?"

"No change, sir. That Injun is still stomping and whooping it up. The off-duty men are standing around enjoying it. They got a company bet going on what time he makes his big charge." Schmerd dug in his blouse pocket. "I got an extry ticket, sir. Only one dollar. It's for eight p.m. That's a good ticket, Captain. He'll have to go about then, or his legs'll be wore plumb off."

"Schmerd, shut up!" Strinker was in no mood for sweepstake tickets on the hour of Yellow Nose's attack. "Where's Blemmish?"

"Right outside, sir. He's relieving me on guard of the cellblock, sir. I ain't had my supper yet."

"Get back as quickly as you can," ordered Strinker. "I wish to God we had some more non-commissioned men. If only Sergeant Mehaffey hadn't been shot last month. Where's Surgeon Hummerbund?"

"Still over to the hospital, sir. Fixing up them troopers as Bleek broke apart in the store. A couple, four or five of them's got busted bones, sir."

"On your way over to the mess, stop by and tell Hummerbund I want to see him. I don't feel well."

"You don't look too good, neither, Captain; I'll surely send the doctor right along for you, sir."

"Get out!"

"Yes, sir, just going, sir. May I compliment Lieutenant Funder on the way he handled the fight, sir? He was surely impressive on the field."

"Schmerd—!"

"Oh, of course, Captain, he wasn't nothing like you'd have been, happen you hadn't of gone for coffee."

"Sergeant!"

"Yes, sir, but what I meant, sir, was that the Lieutenant, he certainly did show your grand influence, sir. You're a great trainer of fighting men, Captain, sir. I salute you!"

Schmerd snapped a smart salute and Strinker relaxed.

"Why, thank you, Stanley. Run along and have your supper now. And never mind the doctor. A good commander sees first to the medical attention of his troops, of course."

Stanley Schmerd departed across the darkening parade ground. In his simple heart was a stirring known only to men smitten past repair. Over yonder the winking lights of the company kitchen were not the smoky blurrings of kerosene lanterns but the crystalline coruscations of the farther stars. Within their lumined hall waited for Stanley Schmerd the creature of his innermost desires. They were guideposts to his winged and manure-smeared boots. They led him on over the cigar butts and marbled mule droppings of the parade ground as if through Elysian fields of angel burls and uncut priceless gems of the Orient. Stanley was in love. At the door of the mess hall he paused on toes more lightly trod than those of the prairie hare a-dance in a moonlight circle. The cadence of his knuckles upon the rough-hewn panel was urgent, entreating, impatient with longing unrequited since stolen moments at reveille's bugle, summoning him to soldier's duty the full day since, had sent the sergeant off into the autumn sunrise awash with Katie's coffee and her kisses.

Yet now the doleful-natured croak which answered to his rapping from within would scarce have favored a marsh frog well advanced in lung fever.

And the cause was almost as serious as the sound.

Entering in alarm, Schmerd found his paramour of the morning—and of many a moonlight stroll ere that—in a condition he had sought to inspire in his own behalf within her boundless breast, and failed, these many months behind Mehaffey's back. He found Wee Katie still in swoon from her first sighting of the man from Horse Creek half a day before. But, more than that, he found the delicate thing in a blue-dark mood of despondency, something to do with searching her Gaelic soul to know that she might be good enough for the "foin and daycent grand great red-furred fellow from far out on the prayree."

The problem, Schmerd discovered, when once he had translated her mooings and calfings into human terms, was that Wee Katie was not certain of her status with the Creator.

54

It would never do, she explained to the scowling sergeant, for a daughter of the True Faith to press herself upon any good man of the cloth, even a heathen Protestant, when in her own pure mind Kathleen Mehaffey did not know if she were yet a properly elegible widow woman, or ever could be. When Schmerd then learned that to some degree he himself figured in the Widow Mehaffey's dilemma, he at once ceased glooming over his own poor fate as a seeker for Wee Katie's hand and devoted his crafty-stupid thoughts to his possible status in the eyes of a sterner law than even the Irish matron's.

The fact of the rather messy matter was that the late Dennis Mehaffey, First Sergeant, U.S. Cavalry, was scarce a fortnight in his grave—God rest his roaming soul—and had come to his sudden and ill-timed end in action and with honor in the field. Indeed, Schmerd and Mehaffey had been together in the fight, a running skirmish with some Kiowa-Comanches of old White Bear's bailiwick, and Dennis had been outrunning Stanley until cut down in noble stride by a single well-directed shot from the rear. It was the very idea that this shot had been so dead-center-sped which caused the subsequent rustle of loose tongues in the Larking barracks. It seemed that not all of the two companies of cavalry involved in the clash, which itself was no more than a routine long-range demonstration by the red riders with no heartfelt charges or close-in circling, believed the fatal lead to have been red. Quite a few of the doughty recruits in Mehaffey's company had contended that the notable boom of a trap-door Springfield had preceded the shot which laid fair Dennis low. These same lads had insisted, too, that Mehaffey ought to have been cut into by Dr. Hummerbund, the thought being that the recovery of a .54 caliber Springfield ball from between the shoulderblades of stout Dennis might very well incriminate someone beside White Bear and his war-bonneted braves.

If the autopsy had been done, no report of its findings had exited the post hospital. Talk of the good sergeant having been plugged from behind by one of his own fellows faded for lack of primary evidence. But suspicion lingered in certain quarters, not the least of which, or whom, was in the wily mind and female instincts of Wee Katie herself.

Now, smitten by the twin arrows of her crush on Preacher Bleek and the twingy problem of Stanley Schmerd giving sign of stubborn refusal to leave the field, the pining widow slyly elevated one orange eyebrow toward the muttering Schmerd and emitted another of the hoarse cowfrog croaks.

"Stanley, me boy," she boomed, "yez know, there's something I've always meant to inquire of yez, relating to the demise of me late husband, Dinnis; jist where was yez whin the brave boy was strick down? 'Tis said about the barracks that yez fired but wan shot in the whole fraykiss, and that wan at no Injun, since none was nearer than artillery range."

Schmerd put down his coffee cup, bugging out his small rodent's eyes. He had a very cunning look for Wee Katie.

"Why, Kate, my love," he smiled. "Whatever can you mean?"

"I could mayne," shrugged the lady mountain of the Plains, "that yez murthered me dear swate Dinnis, so's yez could get the favors of his faithful helpmate, which same yez niver could come by on yer own, yez miserable spalpeen!"

"Ah, now," nodded Schmerd, ferret's glance checking the room and all windows for possible witnesses, "surely you ain't aiming to impune that I done any sech of a cowardly and daspherous deed, for serious, Mrs. Mehaffey?"

"It ain't me suggestion," shrugged the freckled widow. "But, faith, I'm wondering whut the Inspector Gin'ril's lads would think of it, should the weeping widdy woman, her-ownself, supply the possibility. Do you rickon, now, Stanley, me boy, they would order thimselves a post-mortimus on the remains?"

Schmerd's puttied features sagged and grew ugly. "Curse you!" he growled, getting up and backing away from the table. "Do you aim to threaten me, Kate, you she-devil?"

"Ah, now!" pounced Wee Katie. "Would an innycent man call it threatening, Sergeant dearie?"

"You witch!" said Schmerd. "What is it you want of me?"

"Only that yez kape clear of me and the Praycher," replied the creature of his desires. "Layve us be, utter and absolute, and kaype yur murthering nose to yerself. Have we a dayle, Stanley darlin'?"

Schmerd glared at her. If looks could commit such things, Wee Katie would have been dead as she stood in her brogans.

"We'll see!" he said, and stormed back out into the night.

# 10

IN PREACHER's cell all seemed serene. In the neighboring cell the Horse Creek children slumbered the sleep of the just—or appeared to. For his part, Preacher was content to leave them at rest. Upon his burdened mind, if not reflected in his outward calm, much weighed which needed tending. Of immediate heft was the matter of the absent garrison troops. Bleek had made discreet inquiries of his two guards, a pair of scoundrels who had joined the army to permit certain legal warrants to expire back home, and had learned that the commanders of the two hay and wood details were lieutenants he had known up the Arkansas. In neither case was the absentee officer to be trifled with. Both were West Point men and of the type to whom discipline and duty were sacred. The return of either would spell certain darkness for the hopes of Preacher Bleek and his orphans of the Horse Creek school to escape Fort Larking and whatever fate awaited the children at the hands of the Indian Bureau. As to the Washita children presently residing with Mrs. Kathleen Mehaffey at the post mess hall, God alone could tell their fate should Preacher fail to extricate them from the frightful jeopardy into which he had innocently plunged them with his search for good Major Kindthorpe and that U.S.

58

Cavalry escort to Smoky Hill. So the issue came squarely down to one conclusion, and Preacher understood full well its shape: he must get out of that Fort Larking guardhouse and get those Indian children—all of them— back to their own people before the absent troops returned.

Ah, but how?

Bleek was a powerful man. But an engineer of frontier experience had built that jail on the Kansas post. Its mud and stone and sodden log walls could not be burned, nor burrowed, nor broken through. The only way out of that prison was by superior brain power, and no one knew better than Preacher his woeful lack in this direction.

However, there was always the Lord.

Bleek went over to the window of his noisome cage. He drew a deep lungful of the sweet praire air wandering in from the moonstruck sage, rabbit-berry bush, and aromatic yellow willow of the river bottoms. Lord God Almighty, but freedom out there was the only life, he thought. The idea that he had brought his little ones, and the innocents from the cavalry fight on the Washita, so near to the loss of this priceless gift which was their outland birthright, made his heart plummet yet deeper within his great breast.

"Dear Lord," he began, "bring me some inspirement that I may know you ain't deserted your servant Nehemiah. Things has come down to a fearful pass whereat I got to depend on my wits to grease me and them pore small kids out of this here wicked bastion of the Philistines. Now, Lord, you know that heavy headwork ain't my primariest salvation, and I—"

Bleek broke off, tiny blue eyes narrowed upon a nearby rise of prairie distinguished by three sentinel cottonwood trees. Beneath those trees a campfire bloomed like a rambler rose of the night. By its warmth, Preacher knew, squatted five Cheyenne of rank among their people, both in war and in statesmanship. He imagined, too, that the spirits of these five warriors would be in need of some unguent scarce supplied by their lonely blaze outside the walls of Fort Larking, Kansas. Preacher turned his homely face upward.

"Thank you, Lord," he nodded. "I knowed you wouldn't come up short on me."

# 11

THE WIDOW MEHAFFEY had no knowledge of and less respect for the messages of a non-Roman Jehovah. An eminently practical woman, possessing, too, a libido in proportion to her other dimensions, she only understood that on this earth first things come first. It was thus that Preacher had an unexpected visitor to his cell before he might implement the word of the Lord.

"Faith, now," he heard her voice in the outer office of the guardhouse, "and would I be after caring for the orders give to the loikes of yez two hangdog scuts? Out of me way, yez whimpering puppies!"

Bleek heard soldier curses, then the sounds of bodies being tossed aside and into hard walls and down upon an equally unyielding floor of rammed earth. With that the outer door of the cellblock was flung open and, framed in the smoky yellow light of the office lantern, Preacher had his first vision of the lovely Kathleen Mehaffey. Simultaneously, he was treated to a personal second helping of the voice which he now was able to catalog as midway twixt that of the lesser Arkansas bullfrog and the call of the she-grizzly in oestrus.

"Ah, Praycher darlin', there yez be!" announced Wee Katie, billowing into the cellblock, followed by the

61

bruised and abused troopers of the guard. "And would yez be after being good enough to help out a poor widdy woman as is fair-new at nursing injun waifs, Praycher dear? Shure and the little toikes are a'pining and a'whining over yonder to me kitchen something fit to curl the braids of a Pawnee buck. They're a'starving to dith, Praycher, but they won't touch a crumb of the lovely meal I fixed for thim. I'm that feared, sor, that they're a'yelping for homesickness, do yez see, lad, and I wuz wondering, now, if yez would give me the saycret wurd in their haythen tongue to make the little divils ate?"

Here the two troopers tried again to lay hands to the Widow Mehaffey, and again were swept aside like swarming meddlesome flies. Preacher, at first alarmed by the sight of so much female—he was by nature a man deep-feared of the fair sex—knew a moment of admiration now. It was as though the display of overwhelming yet modestly employed strength wrought some other bond than that of Eden between Nehemiah Bleek and Mrs. Dennis Mehaffey. Preacher steadied notably.

"Madam," he said, "You'd best not clout them two again. They'll mayhap get a mite of sense knocked into them, and I cain't afford no smartened-up guards. Boys, you'd best stand clear of the lady," he told the two troopers, as they staggered back to their feet. "The mark of a real soldier is to know when to give ground. If you two will just trot back out to the front office, now, me and—" He paused, reaching for the name of his visitor, and Wee Katie opened upon him a dazzlement of fine white Irish incisors which would have blinded a less simple fellow.

"Mrs. Dinnis Mehaffey, Praycher darlin'," she smiled. "But yez can call me Kathleen."

"Thank you, Mrs. Mehaffey," bowed Preacher stiffly. "I reckon you can call me Nehemiah, coming to that."

62

"Boys," scowled Wee Katie, "didn't yez hear the Praycher? Evapyorate, yez sneaking jackals. Or must I report yez to Sarjunt Schmerd for abandoning yur post of jooty during a stayte of wor?"

The soldiers exchanged scowls of their own. Perhaps the outer office was a safer post to walk, at that. Moreover, Schmerd was overdue from his supper and just might not approve of finding no one on watch when he came in. As to Wee Katie, every man on the post knew where Schmerd spent his off-duty hours, and in what plump pursuits.

"All right," grumped the brighter of the twain. "But we'll be right outside. None of your tricks, now, Kate."

"Be off wid yez!" waved the widow.

When she was alone with Bleek she tried first to seize his hand through the bars. There was no rapport of swifter achievement than that established by just the right hand-squeeze and dip of the roving eyelash. But Preacher was as shy as a prairie mustang; he withdrew from the extended tender trap with a snort of alarm. Galloping to the far, dark corner of his corral, he crouched there trembling and blowing.

"Ah, well, now," surrendered Wee Katie, and turned artfully from the mating game to the lesser business of her night call upon Preacher Bleek. When the latter plainly understood that the wild Cheyenne children were sulking in their fine warm quarters, he was sore-worried for their health. An appeal for parole to Schmerd, who just then arrived for purposes of returning with Mrs. Mehaffey to the mess hall, was of course, and summarily, denied. Stanley Schmerd may not have been a college man, yet neither was he without that certain element of native wit requisite to survive in a competitive society. What! give official sanction to a stroll across the moonlit parade ground shared by this out-sized preacher and his glimmering own Kathleen Mehaffey? Did the twain of them consider Stanley Schmerd a clod of barren intellect? Ha! And, ahah!

However, the sergeant was mollified when the patient and slow-witted Bleek explained that the same message he himself had intended to convey to the pining Indian children could be taken to them by Red Dust, the elder of his own brood. Surely a man of Sergeant Schmerd's patent good sense and rare soldier's judgment could not object to one Indian child being dispatched upon an errand of Christian mercy to a group of his own blood and tender years?

Naturally, Stanley Schmerd was no such beast. The boy could go, provided that Bleek could furnish one good reason for his selection as messenger. It was not that the sergeant was a suspicious man, but the Reverend must understand he had his duty and would have to file a report.

Preacher then said that Red Dust was himself one of the wild Cheyenne, a northern boy from Wyoming some years ago come to the Horse Creek school. The survivors of the Washita would listen to him where they would not hear of orders borne by Blackbird, Buzzard, Sunflower, or the others.

Satisfied, Schmerd unlocked the neighboring cell and brought out the Cheyenne youth.

"Mahesie," instructed Bleek, using the lad's native name and tongue, "you must tell the wild children to eat and to obey the round white squaw while in her lodge. Be careful. Do not try to run away. Remember, Preacher will bring you away from this place in safety. Tell that to the other children, too."

Red Dust made the respect sign of his people, touching

64

the fingertips of the left hand to the forehead. "I will do it, Preacher," he said. "Be careful yourself."

By way of precaution, Schmerd ordered the two troopers in the outer office to go along as escort to the Cheyenne youngster. Pleased enough, the soldiers marched away over the parade ground. One held Red Dust by a rope fastened leashwise about the boy's neck. The other kept his rifle, not on the Cheyenne courier of Preacher Bleek, but on the rolling form of Mrs. Dennis Mehaffey. In this way they came to the mess hall and the post kitchen, and the wild children, heartened by Red Dust and the word from Preacher, fell to and ate like young starving wolves.

As for the boy, Mahesie, whose name meant Red Dust or Red Earth, he felt a sense of race pride and warrior blood surge through him at the success of his entrustment.

In all of the Cheyenne people there was no higher nor more noble blood than that in the veins of the small, very dark-skinned northern boy. He was the full nephew of the vaunted fighting man, Roman Nose. It had been the latter, indeed, who had brought him to Bleek's school from his home in far Wyoming, charging Preacher with teaching this last of a great Cheyenne line the ways of the white man.

Mahesie still pined for his famed uncle. He was still homesick in the dark hours of each night for his homeland in the pines and snowpeaks and upper plains. But Roman Nose, since lost in war, had said that he must stay with Preacher, and Red Dust had agreed and so he had stayed. Now he had done a small thing for Preacher, and in that way for his uncle, and he was content and knew peace for the moment.

As for Mrs. Mehaffey, the immediate manner in which the wild foundlings responded to Preacher Bleek's message only served to increase the burden of her ardor for Nehemiah; and grandly, with that, to enlarge the area of her general charity. With a bit of an Irish curtsey and a 200-pound taptoe of a Kerry jig, she shone upon the two startled escort guards like the misty moon of Galway rising o'er the bay.

"Faith, now, lads!" she trilled. "And what's yur hurry? Grab a chair and have yurselves a platter of me special Injun stew. Should Stanley darlin' say a blissed wurd, yez need only tell him that 'twas Mrs. Dinnis Mehaffey as was after asking yez to stay. Shure and he'll git the pint."

The feckless pair, nothing loath to augment their bully beef and grayback hardtack with a ladling of Irish-Cheyenne mulligan, set to and did the army proud.

Seeing only that the louts were well started, Wee Katie made a sign behind their backs for Red Dust to follow her out of the room. The Cheyenne youth started to do so, but forgot the rope which bound him to the first trooper. The sharp tug pulled the man away from a spoonful of stew, his teeth snapping on empty air. With a curse he leaped up and seized the rope. Katie, however, was ahead of him still.

"Why, see there," she said. "He wants to go outside."

"I'll knock his Injun ears loose," growled the man, drawing back a hand. Kate moved in, all motherly graciousness.

"Lah!" she exclaimed. "And don't yez know these red whelps has got to be took out the very same as inny other animile? Give me that leash, yez ninny, and get out of me way. The crayture is naught but a child of nature. I'll jist walk him about, whiles yez lads lap up yur supper."

The soldiers scowled, then nodded and returned to their plates. Kathleen Mehaffey took Red Dust by his rope and led him out into the kitchen yard. Once free of the line of sight through the open door—which the soldiers had demanded—she grasped the Indian boy by the nape of his neck and whisked him around the corner of the building.

"Listen, yez red cub, yez!" she ordered through clenched teeth. "I know fur a fact that yez understand the King's blinking English, see? So don't be after telling Katie Mehaffey that yez don't! Yez hear me, Rid Dust?"

The Cheyenne boy, if he did or did not comprehend her hoarse whispers, nodded to signify that he did.

She eased her grip, patting him on the tousle of his raven-black hair. "Lad," she smiled, "yez and yur rope take off now. Gallop over to the winder of Praycher's cell and tell him that Mrs. Mehaffey—his own devoted Kathleen—is a 'holding the two guardhouse so'jers over here to the kitchen. Advoise the darlin' that if he's to make a move, he'd best be about it the whiles he has only that murthering dog of a Stanley Schmerd to worrit over."

Red Dust frowned, then reached out in the darkness and shyly returned the headpats Mrs. Mehaffey had given him.

"Round White Squaw heap good man," he assured her, in his proudest version of her own tongue. "Me do."

With that, he was off through the night. Turning, Wee Katie went back into the warm fragrance of her kitchen. The troopers at once noted the absence of Red Dust, but she blushed and told them that his business in the yard had been of a more compelling necessity than she had first imagined. However, the men were to be certain that all was amply secured. The lad was not only tied to the seat of the outhouse shanty, but the stout door with its hand-cut half-moon was also shut and barred by its outside hasp. The dear tad was to sing out when he was ready to return and in the meanwhile it would be only the least morsel of Christian compassion to permit him the solitude of his meditations.

Since this suggestion came laced with two steaming cups of black coffee, and the coffee laced with two steaming shots of Old Crow from the Mehaffey house-jug, the doughty minions of the post guardhouse agreed to consider the situation.

But the first soldier was a mean fellow, and a churl.

He downed the whiskey and the coffee in one gulp, then wiped his leaking mouth with the back of one hairy hand and leeringly allowed that he would just amble out and see for himself how busy things were at the Halfmoon House.

Mrs. Mehaffey paled a trace but recovered in less time than it took the soldier to reach the kitchen door. Seizing up his companion from the table, she thrust him also out of the exit in the tracks of his fellow. In a whisk, she was around and ahead of both of them, pointing out the winding path that they might not stumble and bark their duty-bound shins, or worse.

Reaching the hallowed rest, the first trooper, his pal peering hard at shoulder, ripped open the heavy plank door.

"By God, I knew it!" he roared. "It's empty!"

"Oh, no it ain't, yez lying sots!" roared Wee Katie, and shoved both rascals into the outhouse and bolted shut the iron hasp behind them. "Swayte draymes," she hallooed through the drafty cracks of the whip-sawn planks. "I'll layve yez out in the marning, lads. Rist easy the while."

# 12

WITH MRS. MEHAFFEY gone, Preacher rubbed his two hands together and smiled his simple smile of goodwill. He would now proceed upon the Lord's business, interrupted by the arrival of the large Irish woman—rather, the short and strong Irish lady—no, be honest, it was the somewhat ample and extremely shapely Irish widow—ah, well, in any case, the inspiration sent him by the Lord in answer to his prayer at the cell window could now be implemented.

But once more the Lord's work was delayed.

This time it was the sound of Sunflower sobbing quietly in the next cell. When Preacher went to the intervening bars and called softly to know the trouble, the little Arapaho girl came to the bars and said that she was unhappy because Lame Wolf, the great long-coated guardian of the Argonaut, had not been fed his supper. He would be hungry, and, moreover, he would be lonesome for Sunflower, who loved him best.

Preacher reached through the bars and stroked the child's shining dark hair. His hand was soft in its touch as a mother's. "Listen," he whispered, "don't you know that there old wolf is tough enough to go a hundred nights without his supper, honey? Why, you can bet he ain't one jot hungered. Not yet, he ain't. And we'll have him fed right off, anyhow. Ain't Preacher told you that he'd have the lot of us out of jail and rattling on our way in the old wagon 'fore the moon sets this night?"

It was a lie, most likely, but Preacher knew the rules of living in a child's world. They must not lose hope, not ever. The idea of being free and happy once more was something as important as food. No, it was more important. If a man lied to make a child smile and go back to sleep, well, the Lord would figure out some way to make it balance.

Sunflower now accepted the giant's simple tale, patted his thick fingers and kissed them quickly. Preacher felt the warm salt of the tears through the silken brush of the soft lips, and his heart grew small with hurt, shrinking in his huge chest to the feel and squeeze of a stone.

He turned away from the bars and little Sunflower, more determined than ever to make the Lord's message of hope a real harbinger of freedom for his red foundlings.

He put his eyes and full brainpower to concentrate on the object Jehovah had shown to him in the flash of light which followed his cell-window look at the distant prairie camp of the disgruntled five friends of Yellow Nose.

The object was the pot-bellied iron woodstove which stood in Preacher's cell to heat the entire prison area of the cellblock. Alongside the stove was a plentiful supply of cut wood. On his cell's tier of bunks were ticking mattresses stuffed with chicken feathers, horse clippings, torn newspapers, dried buffalo hay, and no doubt a few chips, all splendid materials for Preacher's purpose. There was a third ingredient to the project, necessary to it, that was; and Preacher had that to hand, also. Praise the Lord!

When jailing the Horse Creek missionary and his dark-skinned flock, Lieutenant Funder, no martinet like

Strinker, had permitted certain personal effects of Preacher and his band to be brought into the cellblock and piled in the corner of Preacher's cell. In the pile were such out-country housekeeping items as buffalo robes, stolen army blankets, spare dry-moss leggin inserts for Little Chief's problem, certain toiletries of the Indian kind, a sack of rock candy which Preacher always carried on his journeys for quelling juvenile disturbances—he would either dole out its contents or use the bag as a blackjack, whichever was required—and a variety of other things which Preacher had not itemized for the guards, but rather had secreted in the blanket rolls.

In addition, he had his saddle, which he never abandoned, his canteen, powder horn, medicine kit, and warbag.

Now, still smiling, the big man headed for the corner pile. Checking the children and the outer corridor to be sure he was not observed, he reached down and picked up the ancient brass-bound powder horn. Unscrewing its cap, he raised the horn to his lips and drank deeply of its contents. Which, by the bye, was neither black nor granular, although it no doubt would explode if ignited. He was in mid-gulp only, when a small Cheyenne voice piped up from outside his cell window.

"Preacher, for shame—Sweet Jesus is watching!"

Bleek strangled, coughed, fought for breath, spewed into the smoky lamplight a vapor of red-gold spume. He was still gasping for life when Sergeant Schmerd rushed in from the outer office.

"Here, here!" accused the ever-alert senior guardsman. "I seen you! What's going on in here?" His beady eyes darted from Preacher around the cell and back to Preacher again. During the trip, Bleek had time to slip the powder horn beneath his Indian vest of horsehide and porky quills, but Stanley Schmerd was old at the frontier prison game.

He tilted up his bulbous nose, scenting delicately the heavy air of the cell.

"By God, I knowed it!" he announced in triumph. "You snuck in some rotgut! Phew! That stuff must've been bottled in a buffler waller."

He called out for his companion of the guard detail to join him, and Blemmish came in on the trot, carbine barred.

"Edward," said Schmerd, "cover me; I am going into Mr. Bleek's cell. He has smuggled some evil whiskey past the Lieutenant's good Christian charity."

"Yes, Stanley," answered the corporal. "The brute!"

Schmerd unlocked the door, went to the pile of duffle in the corner, and swept up the battered canteen, which was clearly stenciled on its dented side, *Property U.S. Army, Third U.S. Cavalry, Fort Apache, Ariz. Terr.,* but which, since Stanley Schmerd could not read, may as well have been lettered in Sanskrit. However, he knew government property when he saw it, and now accusingly reminded Bleek that the canteen, as well as containing contraband liquor, no doubt had cost some brave soldier boy his life in some foul Indian ambush or other.

His triumph was of brief span, and soured.

When he uncorked the canteen and up-ended it, what splashed out upon the jail floor was pure mountain water scooped from some sandy shelving shore of the Mother Arkansas.

"You devil!" he yelled at Bleek, and tore the corner pile apart, but found no other single container which could have harbored whiskey and so was forced to retreat up the cellblock corridor cursing and threatening the preacher with solitary confinement next time.

When he was gone, and after quieting the re-awakened children, Bleek rushed to the cell window, a-sputter.

"Red Dust, you spying sneak!" he hissed into the outer darkness. "Stand up and be seed like a man!"

In response, the sober-faced northern Cheyenne boy rose up from the night, his handsome face framed by the bars.

"*Hau*," he said, unsmiling. "Me come in peace."

"Aarrr!" growled Preacher helplessly. "You'd be coming in pieces, all right, happen I could get my hands on you! If they's anything I cain't stand, Red Dust, it be a sneak."

The Cheyenne boy nodded, made the Indian sign of respect, turned to go. "Me sneak back, then," he said. "No give you message from Round White Squaw."

"No, wait, you Cheyenne cub! A message?"

The boy gave Preacher the words entrusted to him by the Widow Mehaffey. Preacher was touched by the lady's soft heart and stout goodwill. He instructed Red Dust to return quickly, so he would not be missed and an alarm sounded.

"Listen, lad," he explained, "the Saviour has done answered me when I prayed for him to show us a way out'n this fort. The Round Squaw is trying to help me by keeping those soldiers over there to the kitchen. If you do all you can to side with her, likely I can pop us out'n this Big Iron Cage and we'll all set sail for Smoky Hill River in the wagon."

Red Dust stood tall on the top of the rainbarrel beneath the prison window. He swept the interior of Bleek's and the children's rude cells with a flowing Cheyenne gesture.

"No need talk Injun-talk me," he answered haughtily. "Him no 'Big Iron Cage.' Him 'Lousy Damn Jail.' Me hear soldier say name to Fat Cook Lady."

"All right, all right!" cried Bleek. "For God's sake, be

gone with you. And don't call that fat lady a fat lady, you hear?"

If Red Dust did hear, he returned no sign. He was already disappearing into the moon-silver of the parade ground, trotting toward the twinkling lamplight of the company mess building.

"Ah," breathed Preacher softly, homely face upturned and asking it humbly, "guard the lad good, Maheo." He paused, simple features contorted in the toil of thought. "And, listen," he added, still looking upward, "if that don't tax you too heavy, lend me and the Lord a hand with this here pot-bellied stove."

# 13

PERHAPS BLEEK's Christian Creator resented being put to work with Red Dust's heathen Maker. In any event, when Preacher went back to the pot-bellied stove, he was once more frustrated in his attentions to it.

This time the interruption was supplied by Little Chief.

"Beee-yaawWW!" yowled the small wet brother of Sunflower, the suddenness and spirit of his outcry testing even Preacher's granite nerves. But he was not complaining of dampened pants on this occasion. What disturbed his Arapaho slumbers was a blood-cousin of the same malaise which had earlier seized his sister. Little Chief was just taken with the prairie-quaking thought that his favorites, Black Samson and spotted Delilah, had not been given their night-halt nosebags. "Beee-yaawWW, beee-yaawWW." How could the beautiful mules ever make it alive through the long darkness without their rolled oats and bran? "Beee-yaawWW, beee-yaawWW, beee-yaawWW!"

Could Preacher have snared him through the bars, he might have strangled him. As it was, his caterwauling brought all the others wide awake and inside of three seconds the entire band was ki-yiying at top lung over the sorrow of the foodless mules added to the tragedy of the supperless wolf dog.

The sound gathered itself into a hideous ball of noise and, blasting through the cell's bars, rolled down the jail corridor toward the open door of the outer office.

In that doorway, chair cocked back, boots propped against door jamb, Sergeant Stanley Schmerd dozed with a sawed-off shotgun in his lap. When the collective and multiplied yowl of the Indian children struck him, Schmerd became galvanized. He went up off the chair like a startled cat, eyeballs extruded, hands clutching for empty air. The shotgun, leaping from his unclenched grasp, struck the floor butt first and both barrels went off. The charge of heavy shot sent ceilingward hit the hanging lamp of the office and brought it down about Stanley's shoulders as he lighted on the floor, plunging the office into blind-blinking darkness.

From his post outside the office, Corporal-of-the-Guard Edward A. Blemmish heard the booming discharge of Schmerd's gun and saw the lamp fall and shatter. With no thought for his own safety but full fear for his friend's life, brave Blemmish charged through the jail's front door, into the black office. He was in precise time to collide, head-on, with Schmerd, who was just staggering to his feet. Each thinking the attack by the other to be that of the enemy, both men fell to flailing in soundless desperation at one another, rolling and gasping about the floor with life itself at stake.

In his guardroom annex off the front office, Second Lieutenant Cumpston Funder started up on his rude cot with a snort of wildest alarm. Aroused from a fitful doze on his duty post, Funder had no inkling what combat was being wrought in the office. He only knew that Captain Strinker had assigned him this duty of responsibility for the prison guard, with threat of military ruin for any failure. In this view, no course remained to the gallant lieutenant but that he spring from his cot and charge the darkened room next to his.

But first a slight and reasoned caution.

Let there be light.

Sweeping up the deeply trimmed lamp from the stand next to his cot, he flared its wick to full elevation, leaped for the scene of the animal panting and striving, going forward to seeming death within the pit-black maw of the adjoining room.

With a squeak of command authority, he protruded just his long nose and peering pale eyes into the outer office, casting the lance of his lamplight before him.

The smoky beam fell upon the powerful hands of Sergeant Stanley Schmerd engaged in beating the hapless head of Corporal Edward Blemmish against the unyielding hardpan dirt of Fort Larking's guardhouse floor. As the beam took him, Schmerd squinted up and saw the familiar ratlike face behind the lamp.

"Don't fear, Lieutenant, sir!" he called. "I've got the dastardly devil!"

Funder seemed to grow a foot in height. From rodent the features turned to lion.

"Fool!" he piped, taking one long gliding stride into the now-safe office, and striking pose with lamp on high. "You have Corporal Blemmish there. Release him this instant."

Schmerd, peering down at his prey, recoiled in horror.

"Oh, Edward!" he cried. "Speak to me; it's Stanley!"

Blemmish was in no condition to stand inspection or to answer interrogation. Funder ordered Schmerd to prop him up in the office chair and to follow him, Funder, into the cellblock. There, with the Indian children still yipping, Preacher Bleek apologetically conveyed to the lieutenant that the uproar could not be diminished until some method of feeding the wagon teams and the wolf dog might be arrived at by negotiation between the army and his orphans.

Funder pooh-poohed this possibility, but, at a wave from Preacher, very like the graceful gesture of an orchestra leader, the Cheyenne band tuned up another notch. The thin-pitched wailing was far more effective than any ancient Chinese water torture or puny threat of bamboo burning beneath fingernails. It was simply not to be withstood, in a reference of retained sanity, by the human ear.

The cavalry gave in, if only after four sharp footstomps.

"Plague it!" whimpered the young officer, kicking at the earthen floor a fifth furious time, "it simply is not fair, Bleek. You don't fight like a Christian or a white man. You're a beast, sir, a positive brute. Oh, dear!"

"Yes sir," agreed Bleek. "Now what terms did you have in mind, Lieutenant? Mind you, no shilly-shallying."

But Cumpston Funder was in no mood for delay. When informed that Fleeb and Canister, the two on-duty guard troopers, had gone across the grounds in escort of Mrs. Mehaffey and Red Dust, he first ordered Schmerd, then Blemmish, to take the Arapaho girl Sunflower to the prairie schooner as official observer of the animal feeding. But a winceful look at each bruised hero, in turn, Blemmish having now tottered in to stand at the ready outside Bleek's cell, convinced him he had no one left save himself with whom to entrust such a delicate mission in the field.

Schmerd and Blemmish fought valiantly to change his mind.

Neither hero wished to be left with Bleek and the Horse Creek band.

78

But Funder was resolute when aroused.

He took Sunflower by the hand and departed the cell-block looking neither to the right nor to the left nor in any degree behind. A proud man, Cumpston Funder. It made Bleek's eyes water-up just to see the fine square set of the lad's shoulders and the flap of his shoulder straps marching away through the lampshine of the outer office.

Yet once he was gone, and Schmerd and Blemmish returned to their duties in the outer office, Preacher made haste to repair to his own much-interrupted assignment; the pot-bellied iron stove, and the salvation of his prisoned flock.

While Buzzard and Blackbird, Santiago and Little Chief stared, round-eyed, through the partitioning bars, Preacher fed the old stove new wood until its rusted sides glowed a cherry red. Then, his movements more hurried, more furtive than before, he dragged one of the crude mattresses from the bunkbeds and slit it wide with his skinning knife. Up-ending the gutted pallet, he spilled and stuffed its content of horse hay, feathers, dust, shredded paper, and dried buffalo waste into the roaring stove. With his hockhide winter boots he kicked and stomped the material down on top of the blazing fire, slamming hard-shut the iron door and clanking down its lock-catch fast and tight. At once, the ancient pot began to spit thick clotty smoke from every bolted seam and overlap. "Praise the Lord!" muttered Preacher. And commenced immediately and with the rapt skill of a railway telegrapher to clink open and shut, in its stovepipe seat above the firebox, the damper plate of the wheezing pot-belly.

Indeed, the sounds of the damper's manipulated rhythms were not unlike those of the sending key, nor was the analogy spurious, the connection figurative.

Outside the jail, where its black length protruded through the sagging haunch of the prison roof, the stovepipe from Cell One was wafting upward a distinctly separated fine fat string of smoke signals.

# 14

In the Camp of the Three Cottonwoods, the disparate followers of Yellow Nose sat away the early evening in some discord. Maxemesevoto, Big Baby, was homesick. His self-appointed chaperone Hotomemaes, Dog Chips, grew crotchety with his charge's infantilism. Stick-of-Wood and Fat, known back home along the Smoky Hill as Kamax and Uxtato, squatted side-by-each, blinking through the smoke of the fire the better to glare at one another. Although inseparable comrades in war and peace, they hated one another, or so professed. The other Indian, Hoxaven, Cross Feather, was by a sort of un-spoken begrudgment, voted subchief in the absence of Yellow Nose. Accordingly, he sat alone and a little way off from the others, playing out his role as guardian of the trust left him by Yellow Nose. It was thus that he was the one chosen by Maheo for his side in the strange arrange-ment with the white man's God and Preacher Nehemiah Bleek.

Suddenly the voice of Cross Feather broke ever the bickering of his fellows at the fire. *"Zetōom!"* he barked in Cheyenne. *"Esetovao, enxhotoatovā!"*

"What?" said Fat, leaping to his side. "Smoke issuing in puffs? Where, where?"

"There!" cried Cross Feather, pointing. *"Emenaoeve!"*

"Maheo's tassel!" shouted Fat. "It is coming from the pony soldier fort!"

The others rushed up from the fire. Even Big Baby was excited, and forgot to hold onto Dog Chips' hand. Stick-of-Wood, so skinny he could not waste his strength in excitement, was first to comprehend the significance of the clots of white smoke climbing skyward over Fort Larking.

"That's Cheyenne smoke," he said. "Signal smoke. Which of us will read it?"

One by one, the braves shook their heads. In truth, smoke signaling was becoming a lost art among the fierce horsemen of the Smoky Hill. But at the last moment Big Baby brightened hopefully.

"Say," he laughed. "I just remembered something in the very knife-cut of time; old Yellow Nose, he reads smoke signals like an Apache or a Comanche. Spotted Wolf taught him. That old rascal. He knew everything. Do you know that the great-grandmother, seven times removed, of old Spotted Wolf, was alive in the time when our people were living in the Land of the Mandans, way up in the north country along the Big Muddy River? Ah, that was the time to be a Cheyenne! We were called the Kite Indians then. We had the fastest horses and the most beautiful squaws and our warriors were the—"

"Dog Chips!" shouted Fat in a rage. "If you don't shut that fool friend of yours up in one eye-wink, I will kill him!"

"Yes," agreed Cross Feather. "Please to do that, Dog Chips. This is serious business."

The surly guardian of Big Baby growled that he would quiet his pet, but that there had better be no more talk of killing anyone. When it came to killing, they all knew whose scalp-belt sagged the heaviest.

They did for a fact, and it was Dog Chips', so everyone grew quiet and scowled at the frantically continuing smoke puffs. By the very nature of the smoke's issuance, booming straight up, tinged pink on the bellies by the fire beneath, accompanied even into the night by showers of wood sparks visible even from their vantage on the prairie rise, all understood that the sender of the signals was in dire want of something.

But of what?

And from whom?

And, indeed, by whom was the smoke being made?

Into the straining silence the soft voice of Big Baby came again. "Say," the hulking brave announced, "I just remembered somebody else who understands Cheyenne smoke talk. It surely is funny that I had forgotten *him!*"

"Ha! ha! ha!" snarled Fat, with his ill temper. "Oh, what a funny thing. Shut your mindless mouth, chicken-brain."

"Yes, for the love of Maheo," pleaded Stick-of-Wood, "please be still. Now let us see, that must be Yellow Nose making that smoke. Who else in the fort would know how? But then Yellow Nose would know we have none along to read his message."

"But that is just what I remembered," said Big Baby. "We do have somebody along to read the smoke. Maybe our leader remembered that, too."

"Shut up," said Fat.

"Yes, shut up," agreed the others.

Big Baby, however, was gone back down the trail of memory. In that land his missing mind knew its true home. In that time and in those places passed long ago, the powerful brave's thoughts worked as clearly as any man's. Indeed, no member of the tribe could recall things with the detail Big Baby did. The only trouble was that no one ever cared about those details; no one ever listened.

"Well," said Big Baby, "the funny thing about it is that I forgot myself."

"I wish you would!" snarled Fat.

"Yes," insisted the burly warrior, "you see I used to watch old Spotted Wolf teaching those smoke signs to Yellow Nose. That was great fun, I tell you. Those were the times."

He lapsed into yesteryear, staring emptily but with visible pleasure back into the happier void.

Stick-of-Wood sighed and shook his head and patted Big Baby on the knee. Dog Chips growled softly to the large man and told him it was all right, they all understood. It was left to Fat, a fellow whose mind was as restless as it was irascible, to pounce on the truth.

"Wait but a breath, here," he said, watching the vacant face of Big Baby. "I think the fool has just said something of sense. I think he is trying to tell us that it is he who understands the Cheyenne smoke-talk signals!"

"No!" cried Cross Feather. "The sun will fail to rise first!"

But Fat was right, and the sun would come up again.

Big Baby understood the smoke signals.

"Quickly, then," ordered Cross Feather. "Make a smooth place here in the sand by the spring. Give him a pointed stick and let him write here in this sand what message he reads in the smoke coming from the pony soldier fort."

Dog Chips found a sand-writing stick and gave it to his staring friend, making him comprehend what was wanted of him. Delighted, as always, when his normal fellow-braves found some useful employment for him, Big Baby seized the stick and fastened his intent, if empty, eyes upon the column of white puffs drifting skyward from below.

Shortly, he commenced to make swift sure marks in the damp sand with the fire-hardened writing stick.

His friends crowded forward, leaning down to see what the words were which came from Fort Larking.

The stillness was absolute.

And so was the quality of the message as transcribed by Big Baby: when he had finished his scribblings in the sand and stood up with a flourish of triumph, there was no mark of the several dozen he had made which conveyed any least or slightest sense to his fellow Cheyennes.

"Maheo curse him," rumbled Cross Feather into the leaden silence, "he has done it again."

The others nodded, too unstrung to speak.

But again the cunning Uxtato, the fox-minded Fat, was the equal of the impasse.

"Hold!" he ordered, with the rise of victory in his tone. "He wrote it; he should be able to read it: Big Baby, Maxemesevoto, my brainy brother, you draw with a hand too beautiful for the ordinary eye—please to tell us what is written here in these glyphs of wondrous tongue."

"Oh," shrugged the modest brute, "that is nothing, really. It's Shahi-yena, the language of the ancient people. Spotted Wolf had it from his seven-times removed grandmother, and—"

"Yes, and you learned it from Spotted Wolf when he was teaching it to his foster son, the Ute, Yellow Nose," interrupted Cross Feather. "Very good, big friend. But in the name of the Four Sacred Winds, what does it say?!"

"Oh, that," grinned Big Baby, as if it were the least of it all. "Preacher Bleek is in the big iron cage of the pony soldiers and wants to get out. He wants one of us to come down there and talk with him about the escape. That one will go over the log wall of the fort and thus to the window in the iron cage outside of which stands the water barrel."

"Is that all?" scowled Cross Feather, puzzled. "Just for somebody to come down and talk to him through the iron bars of his smelly pony soldier cage?"

"Oh, he also said the others should come behind this one and meet him later at the gate."

"There should have been more. Try to remember what it was, brother. Bleek is no fool. He doesn't just want somebody to come down there to keep him from being lonely."

Big Baby nodded and frowned with the effort of recall.

"Oh, yes," he said in a moment, "there was one other small thing. Preacher wanted that one of us who came to see him to be the one most near the size of the pony soldier with the three stripes on his sleeve and the very ugly face."

"He means Sergeant Schmerd," translated Fat, proud in his superior knowledge of the white world. "Schmerd is no good, but very big. He was with that devil who replaced good Major Kindthorpe in Colorado. You know, the officer at Fort Lyon who came up to Sand Creek with Chivington?"

Cross Feather said he knew the officer and would admit the sergeant would be no good coming from such a command. But the question here was not a moral judgment of the big white man named Schmerd. Rather, it was the problem of selecting just exactly the best man among them for the mission to aid brave Preacher Bleek, the friend of their people, the protector of their lost children.

The subchief swung his glance upon his four fellows.

"Too skinny," he said of Stick-of-Wood. "Not tall enough and too wide in the buttocks," he decided as to

86

Fat. "Too nasty and too bowlegged and walks too much like a Cheyenne," he ruled for Dog Chips. Skipping over Big Baby, he came to himself with a deprecatory smile and a humility not to be resisted. "For myself," he said, "I am too valuable. Thus it would seem we are left with no choice but a poor one."

"True, true," agreed the good-natured Big Baby. "But whoever is going, I will help him; my heart will go with him each step of the way."

"It will, indeed," Cross Feather told him. "For it is you who are going, empty-head. Get ready."

# 15

PERSPIRING and praying, Preacher kept to his work. The old stove groaned and glowed and sent forth its acrid smoke. And not alone into the night sky over Fort Larking. Soon the cellblock was streaked with layers of the escaped haze, and an advance streamer was snaking along the corridor toward the outer office.

Schmerd, no longer asleep, looked up from his desk by the front door of the office. What the devil was that? Smoke? By damn! it was; and coming from the cellblock.

He sprinted for the corridor. No thought retarded his speed, this time, of consulting with his partner Blemmish. Whatever trouble awaited, Stanley could far better solve it alone than with Edward's help.

Upon surprising Bleek fanning and feeding the stove, the sergeant had no hint of Preacher's purpose, except to assume that he was merely trying to make trouble for Stanley Schmerd. The big ninny knew that Schmerd was in charge, Funder being still away with Sunflower. He was only doing what came natural to Nehemiah, according to the settlers up the Arkansas. And that was making things difficult for his white fellow citizens. Particularly, the pony soldiers.

Yet, Schmerd did have that canny streak.

If that crazy blue-eyed preacher, with his bearskin coat and his mysterious sources of whiskey, thought he was going to lure Stanley Schmerd into that cell—no, wait—perhaps that was the very answer, to go into the cell with the eerie-minded fool and watch him, firsthand. Yes, by damn, that was the solution. Just get Corporal Blemmish to take his post in the outer office, and he would go into the bear's cage with Bleek. That way the Horse Creek preacher couldn't do a thing without Stanley Schmerd being in on it.

Well, that was the coming truth.

Bleek could not have been more pleased, nor have acted more outraged, when the sergeant shouted for the corporal, gave him his orders to take over in the office, and to cover the safe entry and locking-in of Schmerd into Preacher's cell.

For his part, when Blemmish had retired to his new duty post, Schmerd behaved with commendable restraint. He was kind in his words to the curious-eyed Indian children and circumspect in his approaches to Preacher. When the latter suggested a friendly game of cards to while away the hours until daylight, or the return of Lieutenant Funder, Schmerd accepted with a leer. He had a reputation of his own up the Arkansas, and it was for never losing in any game where he had his fair turn to handle the deck.

It was extremely hot in the cell, even with the stove's draft opened wide and the smoke all cleared out of the cell and away from the rooftop by the clean flame of the undampered fire. This may or may not have been a part of Preacher's plan, but it was at least a dividend of importance. Presently the sergeant wiped his red face and bull-neck with his kerchief. "Phew!" he panted. "She's sure warm in here."

"Would you care," asked Preacher politely, "for a wee drop of something to cut the heat?"

Schmerd's baboon-face squinted suddenly at him.

Preacher could virtually hear the cogs and wheels of his companion's self-professed shrewdness turning and squealing for lack of lubricant in the cavalryman's brain.

"Why," said Schmerd innocently, "whatever do you mean?"

"Whiskey," answered Bleek. "Old Crow, five years old, uncut by man or beast."

"You lie!" charged the other.

"I do," said Nehemiah, "when the need arises. However, in this case, the Lord will provide. Seek and ye shall find, Stanley. The trouble be with you, lad, that you don't seek in the right places."

Preacher had arisen and gone to his pile of plunder in the cell's corner as he spoke. Tossing aside the canteen which had earlier deceived Schmerd, he rooted out his old, high-pommeled saddle. Returning with this sixty-pound relic of Old Mexican design and pedigree, he unscrewed the cap of the saddlehorn, revealing it to be threaded to the stem of the horn, precisely in the manner of a cavalry-issue canteen. While the sergeant stared incredulously, the man of peace and piety put the saddle across one thick shoulder, after the manner of a great goatskin winebag, and, with a flourish, commenced to pour from the saddlehorn into the first of the twain of tin cups he had unearthed from the pile, unseen by Schmerd.

Stanley could only gulp and nod and accept his brimming tin of the good golden corn when Preacher handed it over to him. As for Preacher, with his own tankard brimmed, he put the cap of the saddlehorn back on, set the saddle to convenient hand upon the earthen floor, sank back, crosslegged, to that floor and asked quietly of Schmerd, "Whose deal?"

The sergeant looked at him a long moment.

There was more than disbelief, more than respect, mirrored in the wavering regard; there was awe.

"Lord Gawd Amighty," breathed Stanley Schmerd, "real whiskey! And hid in a Spanish saddle's front swell!" He raised his cup, sniffing of the bourbon's effluvia, well released in the cell's stifling temperature. "AhhhhhHH! ambroozhia!" he whispered huskily, and drained the fiery cup at a gulp.

"Cheers," said Preacher soberly, and emptied his own bent tin at a sip.

# 16

BIG BABY went through the night without fear. He was of too simple a mind to know the alarms of his forebears over the shades of the darkness—the forms of the departed Indians supposed to come above the Mother Earth when the sun was gone. Big Baby rather liked the idea of ghosts. A dead one come back might be interesting to talk with, the proposal being that he would know a lot about the old times when the people were a great race of warriors and wise men, and when things were not so complex as presently.

When he came to the stockade, he followed it around to where its log-set jaws gaped to the orifice of the main gate. Here, after a moment of study, he concluded that no one was watching the mouth of the fort that night. Evidently, a celebration of some variety went forward within the compound. Plainly, Big Baby could hear the cross-parade laughs and comments of the pony soldiers, and the whining reel of an eaglebone flute. Aha! that was it; old Yellow Nose was entertaining the troops, and he was doing it so that Big Baby could get into the fort with ease, and also reach the iron cage window of good friend Preacher without any trouble.

Oh, that Yellow Nose! What a cunning little Ute he was!

Big Baby faded through the gate like an outer shadow of the prairie night. It is doubtful that an alert guard walking his proper post at the entrance would have seen the Smoky Hill warrior. Only a closed and barred barrier might have prevented his intrusion. As it was, he was at the wall of the post prison in but another heartbeat. And there he found the cell window of Preacher, as the smoke signals had said he would find it—water barrel and all.

Big Baby sat down on the water barrel. Seated thus, he was comfortably able to lean his elbows on the mud-plastered sill of the window, and place his great face against its bars, the noble nose protruding into the cell some four inches.

"Hello there, good friend," he said in Cheyenne to Preacher. "Did you send for one of us to come see you?"

Preacher was quite naturally startled. He was still at game with Sergeant Schmerd; even if the latter was nearly unconscious from the whiskey and heat, it was yet a trace early for hostile Cheyennes to be talking to Bleek over his weaving head. Schmerd apparently thought so too. He slewed around on the floor, his blurry state trying to focus on the window's revolving bars. "Who's there?" he demanded thickly. "Is that somebody there?"

Bleek, as quick on his feet as a milkweed seedling, wafted his two hundred fifty pounds over to cover the cell window, and to laugh a booming Preacher Bleek laugh and to say that it was only a mule clearing its throat which the soldier had heard. "Forget it, sir," advised the amiable host of Cell One. "It's your deal."

With the assurance, Preacher raised an elbow rearward and smashed the intruding nose of Big Baby back out through the bars, and the wounded brave made a sound like that of a large snake run over by a loaded wagon.

"What was *that?*" demanded Schmerd, weaving to his feet.

"Ah," said Preacher Bleek, "I do believe I surprised a rat prowling the water barrel. Poor creature. It fell from the sill and will have to swim for it, I fear." Preacher pressed his blunt features to the bars, rolling his deepset eyes to peer downward and outward. "Do you hear me, great stupid clumsy rat!" he bellowed down at the crouching Big Baby in outraged Cheyenne. "Don't peer into my window again until you are asked."

Schmerd sank back to the floor, holding his head. The cell was spinning. Preacher came over from the window and looked down upon him. "You need another drink," he said, and proceeded to mix one from the corner pile of his personal plunder which he believed might climax the night successfully.

Into the tin cup with only enough whiskey to disguise the augmented flavor went an ounce of beaver-gland oil, a finger of Horse liniment, two of screw-worm extract, and a sprinkling of Old Trapper Ant and Roach powder. Swizzling the elixir with his forefinger, Preacher presented it to Schmerd, along with the deck of cards. "Down the hatch," he waved. "One good slug of that, Stanley, and you won't hardly feel nothing solid below your beltline, nor familiar, above. Deal!"

The sergeant steadied the cup with both hands, drained it in drunken faith. Perhaps four seconds passed, during which he did nothing, made no sound, essayed no movement. Then he bounded to his feet with a soundless shriek, forcing Bleek to lean close to hear what he said. Which was to the strangulated effect that he was blind, deaf, mute, and struck dumb, and that Preacher had poisoned him, and would swing for it. With this, he went

94

up on his toes, wiggled all over like a beached trout, wet in the bank-sand, passed out stone-icy-cold and extinct on the rammed-earth floor of Cell One.

Seizing him beneath the arms, Preacher dragged him over to the window. "Now then, you dumb red ape!" he hissed into the outer night, "get up here and do what I tell you!"

The moon face of happy Big Baby rose into the frame of the iron bars, pleased as ever to be wanted. "Take off all your clothes," Preacher ordered him in Cheyenne, "and pass them in the window to me." As he spoke he was stripping Schmerd of his uniform, down to his winter-issue underwear. "Hurry up, hurry up!" he urged the disrobing Big Baby. "We must do this thing quickly, or be discovered."

Big Baby had not the remotest notion of Preacher's plan. But, like all children, he loved to dress up in someone else's clothes. The idea of charading as a sergeant of pony soldiers especially appealed to his simple ego. *Wagh!* Wait until the others saw him in such finery! *Ai!* their eyes would stick out of their skulls when they met him at the gate in another moment, as they were supposed to. Then they would understand that the brain of Big Baby could work well enough when it needed to. They would be proud to be his friends and fellow tribesmen.

By the same token of trust, the big brave handed his own raiment through the bars to Preacher, then listened carefully to the instructions the red-bearded missionary gave to him.

For his part, Bleek also trusted Big Baby.

They were, in a manner of nature, somewhat brothers. If it was said in the Indian community that Big Baby had not the intellect of a sun-fried frog, it was also rumored in the white settlements that Preacher Bleek was mad as a

March hare in mid-August. So the two large men of differ-ent skins, but fraternal minds, smiled now at one another and patted each other on the face through the bars, and Preacher said to Big Baby with all the dignity that was his, "My red brother, I know that you will do it all exactly as I have told it to you. Why do you suppose I sent for you, only? Go now and gather up the others at the gate. From there, permit Cross Feather to lead the way. It will make him happy, and you and I will understand, anyway, that your brain was the important one. *Nohetto,* cousin. Maheo guide you."

Big Baby made the respect sign, and disappeared around the corner of the Fort Larking guardhouse.

He had never felt so fine in his lifetime.

There *was* a man who trusted him!

# 17

"YOU ARE a nice pony soldier. I like you," Sunflower assured Lieutenant Funder, going toward the wagon. "I don't think you would hurt a little Indian girl."

"Of course I wouldn't," snapped Funder. "Be still, and get on with your work. Can I help you?"

"Oh, no. The animals would never permit it."

"How's that?" The note of alarm in Funder's query seemed out of proportion to the small child's statement. Yet Funder had been ill-used that day and was jumpy. "Are you saying they're vicious? The dog is chained, is he not?"

He had stopped at dead-halt, a safe twenty paces from the Argonaut, and was peering toward it through the moonlight. Sunflower smiled her wonderful smile, put her chubby hand in his, and stood close to his booted knee.

"It doesn't matter," she said. "Lame Wolf does as I tell him. He is afraid of me. My medicine is stronger than his."

Funder looked down at her. His hand felt very strange. He had never so much as touched a child, let alone been touched by one. And this limping Kiowa waif was disturbing to him. She was so dirty and disheveled, yet so pretty and soft-voiced and optimistically cheerful. And those eyes!

"Listen here," said Funder peevishly, "how is it that you speak English so much better than the other children? They sound like magpies. Your English is as good as Bleek's. Better, as a matter of fact."

"Yes," said Sunflower proudly. "But that is because dear Preacher taught me so well. I have been his child longer than any other, also. I don't remember another father. My people brought me to Preacher before I could talk any tongue."

"You were hurt? I mean, was that why they brought you to Bleek? I've heard he is a better doctor than most with licenses."

"Preacher can heal a broken stone," announced the Kiowa girl. "Or a bone. Or head. Even a heart, some say."

It was in Funder's thoughts to point out that the Horse Creek medicine worker had not healed the little girl's bad leg, but it was in him even more swiftly that this would be cruel—and the lieutenant was scarcely that.

"See here," he said brusquely, "we are wasting time. Let us get on with feeding these brutes. You didn't say if the dog was chained."

"Yes, he is. Come on, new friend."

When Sunflower's hand tightened upon his, Funder realized for the first time that the child still clung to him. He pulled his fingers from hers. The motion was spasmodic, unthinking. It embarrassed him, made him angry with himself.

"I'm not your friend, little girl," he said stiffly. "I am an officer charged with the responsibility of your arrest. I have come out here purely for reasons of retaining normal control over the jail and its administration. We must do our work here and return as quickly as we may. Hurry, now."

Sunflower nodded and started on, then stopped short.

98

"My name," she said, "is Sunflower. Will you call me that, new friend?"

Funder blushed and stomped his foot. "Yes, yes, if you insist. Go on, please. We must get back."

"All right," she grinned, not moving an inch. "What is your name? We can't get this work done quickly, if we are calling one another 'little girl' and 'new friend.' "

Funder drew himself erect. This had gone much too far. Even if no one was watching. Or would ever know.

He grabbed Sunflower's hand and dragged her toward the wagon, voice gruff. "Look, kid," he growled, "enough is enough. Now you quiet down and get busy!" With the command, he gave her a push toward the wagon's tailgate.

The next thing he knew, a hairy monster was exploding out of the wagon's rear, hurtling through mid-air at his throat. "Look out!" yelled the Kiowa child, and tackled him about the knees, knocking him backward with surprising strength. He lit flat on his back and but an instant before Lame Wolf's great form hit the ground, fangs bared, not three feet away. Sunflower's lunge had saved him. The wolf dog had leaped to chain's end with only inches to spare.

"You see," explained the Kiowa child, brushing off the terrified officer's blouse, "it was when your voice turned angry and you put hand to me. He was watching and he is not supposed to let white men harm Indian children. He's a northern Cheyenne, like Red Dust. That's fighting blood."

Funder regained his feet.

"I think," he said, "I am going to be ill."

"No matter, go ahead," said Sunflower. "I know a great deal about Indian medicine. I will get you something. Where do you hurt?"

Funder groaned. "In my head, I think," he admitted ruefully. "But medicine won't help. Go on, don't worry about me; feed that thing on the chain and order it back into its cave. Ughh!"

Sunflower put pudgy hands to hips, studying him. Shortly, to his startlement, she reached up and felt of his ribs, the stretch made tiptoe. "You know," she said, "you don't feel good to me. You have no muscles, no hard meat, no tough gristle over those bones of yours. Why don't you come and live with Preacher and us out on the prairie? Do you know that when Blackbird came to live with us he was so weak he could not walk to clean grass for his needs. We had to carry him. Look at him now. He whipped two pony soldiers in the store today. All by himself. And he is only twelve years old. Maybe even ten. It's not too late for you. What do you say? I will speak to Preacher about it, if you give the word. He listens to me, too. How about it?"

"Oh, Lord," wailed Funder, "will you *please* feed that monstrous dog, little lady?"

"Sunflower, you mean."

"Yes, yes, my God—Sunflower—only do it!"

"You know something, new friend," said the child, "one reason you are so weak is that you talk too much."

"*I* talk too much?" managed Funder in a croak.

"Indeed you do. Here, why don't you take these nosebags and hang them on the mules? Don't touch the Indian mares; they're mean." She rummaged in the possum belly slung beneath the Argonaut and came up with the nosebags for Samson and Delilah, as well as for the Kiowa Ladies. "Oats are in that bag, bran in the other. Three parts oats, one part bran. Don't turn your back on Samson."

Funder groaned again. But he took the nosebags and

filled them to careful order and started with them to the head of the wagon. He paused on the way to listen to the cheery sound of his troopers egging on Yellow Nose and generally enjoying the Chautauqua atmosphere building up on the parade ground in front of the store. He could hear at least two banjoes and a mandolin and a mouth-harp tuning lustily, and some company singing had begun. It was a fine fall night, very warm for the season. With that enormous harvest moon swinging up from the far rim of the prairie, and a stillness of wind almost summerlike in its quiet, even Cumpston Funder could understand the mood of the men. He thought, fleetingly, of stealing up alongside the store building and taking just one peek at the merriment. Then sanity returned. If so much as one of the troopers should discover him sneaking about the post with two nosebags in his hand and a little Kiowa Indian girl on his flank, it would be the end of all chance in command for Cumpston Funder. The best thing for him was to finish his mission and return to the guardhouse—where Strinker had posted him—on the double.

He started on toward the mules, thankful that Bleek had parked the Argonaut in the rear of the store, but that proved the end of the gratitude. Samson would not cooperate, trying to take his arm off with the nosebag still in it. When he leaped from Samson, Delilah bit him unhesitantly in the ham of his left thigh, forcing him to whirl away from her only to present his other flank, before he might think, to Samson again. The black Spanish jack sampled the right leg higher up, including a choice cut of the butt round. Funder burst into tears.

Hearing him, Sunflower was so distressed that she dropped the chain by which she held Lame Wolf to his feedpan, and ran around the wagon to the soldier's aid.

The wolf dog immediately circled the Argonaut from the opposite direction and reached Funder's vicinity before the Kiowa girl did.

Sunflower heard the roar of his charge, however, and cried out all that she could of life-saving advice to the young officer, shouting, "Get to the top of the wagon—!"

How the lieutenant made the jump from solid ground to the prairie schooner's driving box and thence all in the same single motion to the arched topstays ahead of Lame Wolf's clashing teeth was never known.

Sunflower did not see him do it.

All she saw was the nice young one-bar pony soldier chief astride the ribstays of the Argonaut minus his blue trousers and an important portion of his woolly underwear.

She also saw the blue trousers and the piece of the long-drawers which were missing.

That was when she saw Lame Wolf still leaping at the wagon wheel trying to get up at Lieutenant Funder.

She thought the old wolf dog looked very funny with all those pony soldier clothes in his mouth.

But she was glad, too, that the nice cavalry chief had not been permanently injured, and she did her best to cheer him and to make him understand that all was well.

"Don't worry up there," she called to him. "You will be all right, new friend. Lame Wolf always gets sleepy before daybreak some time. I'm going back to see Preacher and my other friends. Good night. I will feed the mules for you."

Funder tried to call her back, but she would not answer.

He could hear her fussing with the mules and the mustang mares, but she had turned Indian on him. In a few

102

minutes he could not even hear that from her, and he was alone with the night and a white-man-killing Cheyenne wolf dog who always went to sleep before daybreak.

Some time.

# 18

CAPTAIN STRINKER could not sleep. What business he had trying to do so at that early hour of the evening might have interested the promotions board. But Strinker was, in fact, hiding. He had nominated Funder for whatever of military disaster might obtain at the guardhouse or the post store, and sought his austere bunk at the BOQ determined to close his eyes to the entire situation.

Dawn's early light would permit of clearer seeing in any event, he reasoned. And tried once more to drift off.

It was no good.

He got up and lighted the lamp. Standing before the only unSpartan furnishing he permitted in his quarters—a full-length French-gilt boudoir mirror—he straightened his rumpled blouse, standing as tall as he might without his high boots to aid the five feet and spare inches which were his natural elevation. Not caring still for the effect, he reached beneath his cot and brought forth a stout wooden packing box. Mounting this, he posed again and was more pleased. Brushing back his lank pale locks, he peered fiercely into the Paris glass.

Ah! there it was again; the "look" which he had so often remarked in himself; the resemblance to that other dash-

ing young Palladin of the Plains, who had received a somewhat luckier shake from destiny than Strinker.

But wait!

Why not show it all? Why not see again the full startling image of fame that was the fate of Julius Strinker?

Glancing furtively about his lime-washed quarters, the
captain tiptoed down off the box and away into a dark
corner where a cardboard wardrobe stood padlocked.
With deft key he opened the closet and brought forth the
treasures which it hid. Donning the wide black hat,
fringed buckskin overshirt, blood-red neckcloth, elbow-
length yellow gauntlets, he pulled on his boots and returned to the box.

Here, he buckled on his saber and waistbelted his big
Colt sixshooter, shook out his thin blond curls, flared up
the brim of the black hat, and struck his hand to the
pommel of the sword.

Magnificent.

The thin lips, tight with the tensions of command,
parted beneath the drooping straw-colored mustache to
reveal the final kindred claim—the widely spaced peg-
toothed smile of the irrepressible "Boy General" of the
Seventh Cavalry.

Strinker's glance of steely-blue, so like the other's,
glinted with sudden, warlike spark. He wheeled adroitly
on the boxtop. "Orderly," he said, voice low and steady
despite the increasing cry of the Sioux bullets ripping
past, "have the band play 'Gary Owen,' if you please." He
spun a quarter turn left-flank, and snapped, "Trumpeter,
sound the charge." Then he whirled full-front once more,
one boot high and crashing down as he shrilled, "Forward, Hoo-oohHH!" flashing his saber to lead the advance.

But it was a short charge.

The lifted boot, coming down a bit too briskly, drove through the top of the packing box. The boards collapsed with a crunch and Strinker disappeared, nearly to his knees, within the remaining frame of the broken podium.

He stood a moment, thus.

It was touch and go if he would commence to weep, or pull his belt pistol and shoot himself, or both.

In the end the tradition for command of the Strinker men prevailed and, sobbing only softly, the captain left his cheerless quarters to go and see whether Mrs. Mehaffey might yet be up, and a cup of her medicinal coffee on brew.

Something might yet obtain.

After all, even Custer had his off nights.

# 19

BLEEK GLIDED from the cell window to the cell door, and looked down the corridor toward the outer office. He could not see Blemmish, but heard the scratch of a quill pen in the sudden stillness, and knew from that that the corporal was awake and not yet relieved. Good. If Sunflower would only employ Funder for sufficient time, and the dazzling Widow Mehaffey detain the two troopers, the Lord's work might yet bear fruit in Fort Larking's guardhouse. "Quiet, little ones," he admonished his peering chicks, and tiptoed past their noses pressed to the intervening bars. He gave each nose a tweak in transit and the owners grinned and clicked their tongues in the Indian manner to show approval of the entire performance, so far. It was good fun to watch Preacher play cards and feed whiskey to the pony soldier sergeant. It was even jollier to see the three-stripe soldier in his underwear, his "come-off skin," as the red children called it. No doubt it would be even finer interest now in whatever it was that Preacher had in mind for a final thing.

In their innocence, the Horse Creek orphans were not misled. Bleek's closing act was a corker.

The plot was to get Corporal-of-the-Guard, Edward A. Blemmish, keeper of the cell block key ring, to enter

Preacher's cell. Now the latter, if barely literate, was also not without a certain dramatic gift. Some wise man had said that no human force existed more destructive than a simple mind. And Preacher had a very simple mind.

Dressing Stanley Schmerd in the Cheyenne warrior buckskins of Big Baby, he painted the soldier's face in the authentic style of the Smoky Hill band, a warlike counter-banding of charcoal paste and lemon-yellow pigment in a zebra pattern. He then secured a pair of horse shears from his plunder pile, and cut Stanley's thick black hair into a fierce single roach up the center of his neanderthal skull. As the revealed and stubbled bone shown somewhat too Caucasian, Preacher gave it an artistic coating of zinc-white, the effect above the black-and-yellow face being precisely right for a war-trailing Cheyenne hostile.

Standing back, Preacher took an earned applause of tongue clicks from his shining-eyed audience. Then, giving the children their cue for entrance into the next scene—the big scene—he drew a deep breath and plunged on.

Dragging the unconscious Schmerd into the center of his cell, he commenced to wrestle with the limp opponent in a most desperate manner, his vast strength permitting him to move both Stanley and himself with amazing real-ism.

At once, the Indian children set up an uproar of yelps for help. A wild savage from Smoky Hill was attacking and killing poor Preacher. *Kiyi! Kiyi! Kiyi!*

Blemmish came on the gallop.

He saw a giant painted Indian atop Preacher Bleek in mid-floor of Cell One. The vicious red man had Preacher by the throat and was banging his head against the hard earth. Preacher was nearly done for, as any soldier could

108

plainly see, and if help were to be in time, it must be swift.

The corporal dropped caution, seized the key ring.

Opening the cell, he raced to Bleek's aid, carbine ready.

But by the time he arrived, the unconscious Schmerd was beginning to come around, stimulated by the rigors of Preacher's calisthenics. Seeing his peril, Bleek shouted for Blemmish to take on the recovering savage, spelling Preacher, who would meanwhile gladly hold the corporal's gun.

Blemmish never faltered in his duty. Surrendering the carbine to the Horse Creek prisoner, he attacked the woozy Schmerd with feeling. Preacher, standing by with the gun, cheered the corporal on, assuring him of fair play. The Indian children were about evenly divided in their sympathies, Buzzard being for the bogus Cheyenne, Blackbird for the underdog white man. Little Chief cast the tie-breaking vote by squalling that he needed immediately to make water.

In this crisis, Sunflower returned from abandoning the treed Lieutenant Funder, and was greeted with great joy and a few light sprinkles by Little Chief. Bleek called to the girl to get the key ring from his cell door and release the waterlogged Little Chief and take him outside. Blackbird and Buzzard, he ordered, would meanwhile get their things together and be ready to go when Sunflower had drained her little brother.

Here there developed some unconsequential delay between the youths. Blackbird was vehemently denouncing Buzzard for championing Schmerd, knowing full well he was only a white man dressed in Indian garb. Buzzard was yelling back that he didn't care, "by Jesus!" and would be for the Indian whether he was red or white.

With no time to arbitrate the distinction, and less to discipline the vain use of the Lord's name, Bleek shouted at top lung for the quarrel to cease and desist, and the boys to do his bidding, or he would leave both of them in the guardhouse jail when he and the others shortly lit out for the Smoky Hill and home sweet home.

Some little of the sense of this shout penetrated the inflamed brain of combat cavalryman Edward Blemmish.

He stopped clawing at the throat of the big Cheyenne warrior long enough for the latter to shake his head free of the final cobweb and inform the fighting corporal that he was trying to strangle his best friend.

"Stanley!" gasped the aroused guardsman. "Who cut your hair?"

If it were a somewhat column-left question, Preacher had a plainfaced frontal answer for it.

"I did," he admitted.

And, reaching down and removing the campaign hat from the corporal's head, he struck him a smart blow across the skull with the butt of his own carbine, replaced the hat unhurriedly and properly, just before Blemmish melted down on top of Schmerd, cold-out as a cindered star.

"No, no!" cried the Indian-clad sergeant, seeing Bleek's continuing intent and trying to struggle from beneath the body of Blemmish. But he was too late. The ironshod butt of the carbine went true again, and Sergeant Stanley Schmerd fell valiantly across the form of his friend, sung also asleep to the ring of warrior-steel in his dizzied ear.

"Children," said Nehemiah Bleek. "Let us flee—"

# 20

YELLOW NOSE was growing very weary. He had danced and blown the eaglebone and chanted the right prayer words for eight hours now, and still no sign had come from Maheo for him to attack.

Besides, the pony soldiers had been treating him very well. When they could see him droop and slow down, they brought him coffee and good fresh water. Or they would clap their hands, as white men did, to urge him on. Even better, a few times some of them had rolled smokes for him with the white man's small fine papers. Ah, those ci-gah-reetes were wonderful—the next best thing the white man had invented, whiskey being naturally the first.

Where the tiny brave had danced, a rut was worn in the dirt of the post roadway. At first this footpath had been scarcely discernible. By noon, it was still no more than two or three inches deep. But, as the day waned and Maheo did not answer, the brave increased the pressure of the dance. By mid-afternoon, he was stomping in a circular recess nearly to the calf. With late afternoon he had worn his way down to the knee and, with sunset, to near buttock depth. Now, at eight o'clock in the evening, he had trenched himself so far into the road that only his head was visible above the wheel ruts.

111

So, to his problems of exhaustion, was added that of a possible self-immurement, definitely not the end which the small chief had had in original view.

The pool-betting among the soldiers had now changed from what hour the Cheyenne headman would charge the post, to what hour he would dance himself underground.

Yellow Nose took a heavy breath, tightened his teeth on the eaglebone flute, prayed devoutly that Maheo was doing something more than was apparent to his child, Heovese, to bring succor to the disappearing war dancer.

His plea fell not on cruel ears.

Over by the deserted main gate, Big Baby was gathering up his faithful comrades and moving toward the post store on the trot. Nearing the troopers surrounding the ceremonial medicine-making dance of their leader, the oncoming braves hesitated only long enough to listen for the eaglebone whistle, and to have its notes tell them that Yellow Nose still danced. They then circled the soldiers, who by now had lighted fires, pitched dog tents, drawn field rations, and in effect set up camp in honor of the visiting Cheyenne war chief, and made their ways like red shadows to the rear of Milch's Emporium.

Here, they were interested to see Lieutenant Funder without his pants sitting on top of Preacher Bleek's big prairie wagon, and Lame Wolf, Preacher's trusted Cheyenne dog, sitting on guard below. But the problems of the pony soldier second-chief were not their problems. And if they were to bring off what Preacher had asked of them, and Big Baby, the visiting Smoky Hill Indians would need all their attention put to their own battle plan.

Briefly, Cross Feather reviewed the strategy as relayed to him by Big Baby. The others all nodded and he waved his hand in the "let's go" sign, and Big Baby turned and loped back up alongside the store, toward the front. At the corner of the building, he stopped running. Trying to walk like a white man, with the toes turned ridiculously outward, he went on around the corner and smartly up to the two troopers on looter-guard at the entrance of Henry Milch's violated store.

On most posts, sergeants of cavalry are not saluted by the enlisted ranks, but these two believed they recognized Stanley Schmerd in the bad light of the overhanging porch roof. Schmerd was a known soft touch for apple-wax, hence the troopers threw Big Baby a proper salute, and the spokesman of the twain drawled, "Good evening, Sergeant; what can we do for you? Some party, eh, Schmerd? Ha, ha, ha."

Big Baby took pause at the unexpected friendliness.

He grinned and bowed and touched the dark fingers of his left hand to his forehead and grunted back in guttural Cheyenne, "*Pavohàzistoz,* yes, a good laugh, ho, ho, ho!" and went on past them into the store, as they drew back, saluting again and nodding stupidly to permit his passage.

It was only after the big Indian had pigeon-toed past them and was three strides into the store that one of them turned to the other, and frowned, "What did he say?"

"*Pavohàzistoz,*" answered his comrade.

"Oh," said the other, relaxing.

Then both soldiers stood up ramrod straight, staring at each other.

"*What?*" they cried in unison, and turned and raced after the vanishing Cheyenne.

It was blinking dark inside the store and the big Indian in Schmerd's uniform seemed to have vanished. But he had really only crouched aside to let them blunder into his grasp. When they were where he wanted them, Big Baby reached out of the darkness and took each soldier by the back of his neck. Raising the two off the floor, he

113

brought their heads together with a ringing crack. This left both of them limp as neck-wrung chickens, and cut off their warning outcry to their comrades outside in the same fashion.

Stuffing the two unconscious troopers into empty flour barrels, heads down and feet crammed in, willy-nilly, the powerful brave left the guards to sleep in peace. At the rear of the store he unbarred the door and admitted his fellow Cheyenne. Scuttling inside, these latter closed the door carefully behind them. "Now, let me see," said Cross Feather. "The first thing Preacher said to do is to hang blankets over that front window. That's so the soldiers can't see what we are doing."

"That's nice," said Big Baby. "But how will we see what we are doing?"

"Stupid one," answered Fat, "we are going to light a lantern as soon as the window is blanketed. That's the whole idea, to permit us to see, yet shut out the eyes of the soldiers. Come on, Stick, you and I will do it."

Stick-of-Wood went to help him, and soon he and the rotund brave had every crack of windowpane snugly covered. "Make the light," said Fat, and Cross Feather did so.

The coal-oil lamp shed a good steady glow. They set it on the counter nearest to them. It was the drygoods and men's clothes counter. "Hah!" said Dog Chips. "The very place that Preacher told us to look for. See there. On those little wooden frames with hooks. All those fine white man's clothes that Preacher told us to dress up in, before we opened the store for business. Come on," he enthused, in a rare display of good nature. "What do you want to be? A farmer? A gold digger? A cowboy? What will you have, cousins? I think I'll be a Tejano, with a big wide hat

114

and some of those high-heeled moccasins with the pointed toes. How about you, friend Big Baby?"

"Hah, hell!" snorted Big Baby, using his one white man's curse word. "I like what I have. A fine pony soldier suit, and I didn't even have to kill anyone to get it."

Stick-of-Wood selected a straw hat and overalls with bib and polka-dotted bandana, like a sod-turner. Cross Feather chose a black sack suit, of a design well-turned for a Philadelphia lawyer, with white dress shirt, gold cufflinks, and yellow spats over his buffalo-hide winter moccasins. He looked stunning. Even if he did wear the cufflinks in his nostrils and breath adenoidally for the rest of the evening.

"Well, hell!" boomed Big Baby, striking himself on the chest. "Let us open the door and do some business!"

Here, Cross Feather smote not his chest but his forehead.

"Ai!" he cried. "I knew we had forgotten something. What is it that Preacher sent us here to sell? By Maheo, it's a good thing I am the leader. It's a good thing Yellow Nose had me to leave in charge. It's a good thing Preacher understood my brain powers, also. By the way," a sudden memory stirred belatedly, "how is Yellow Nose doing out there?"

They all went to the window and peeked out.

"I can't see him," frowned Dog Chips. "All I can see is the dust rising from that deep hole out there in the road."

"But I can hear the eaglebone blowing yet," said Stick-of-Wood. "He must still be dancing down there deep."

"Well, we can't wait for him. Preacher said to do our work no matter if the chief charged the post, or not."

"True, friend Fat," said Stick-of-Wood. "Let's go."

They went back in the store and worked like beavers

for the better part of twenty minutes. They cleared off the hardware counter and restocked the shelves behind it with the other merchandise of Preacher's suggestion. When they had the job done, Fat insisted they must have a looking glass behind the counter, as that was the way that the white men always did a thing like this. The best mirror available was on a lady's ornate dressing table freighted from Kansas City and valued by Henry Milch at $500 gold. Big Baby splintered it free of its cherrywood carved supports and hung it from a stuffed moosehead's antlers to dangle precariously where Cross Feather had stationed himself to wait on the expected trade.

"All right," said the subchief, eying the installation. "We are ready. Big Baby, you know what you must do."

The brave saluted, and slid out the rear door of the store, a supply of the house's best samples under Schmerd's military blouse. Thus it was that two soldiers lounging on the outskirts of the thinning crowd about the site of Yellow Nose's excavation felt a hearty thump on the shoulders from the rear, turned to see the biggest Indian in Kansas history standing there grinning at them from the ambush of a U.S. Cavalry sergeant's uniform.

"*Wagh!*" grunted the Indian. "You pony soldier want buy good stuff heap cheap?"

"I'll cover him, Pete," said the first soldier, reaching for his stacked carbine. "You run and get reinforcements."

"Wait!" ordered Big Baby, spearing Pete with one hand and returning him to the conference, while with the other hand diving inside Schmerd's blouse to bring forth his trade goods. "Me say good stuff, soldier-man. No Injun buffalo water. Look-see him picture blackbird on bottle!"

Both troopers, bemused, peered at the glistening quart displayed by the huge Cheyenne. Surprise and cupidity

116

and a vast unrequited thirst assailed them instantane-
ously.

"Jesus Murphy!" whispered the first man. "Old Crow!"

"Hide it, for God's sake!" said Pete desperately to Big
Baby. "You want every green-manure recruit on the post
to know of the strike? Come on, red brother. Lead the
way. Where's your supply dump?"

"Me show," nodded Big Baby. "But have good friend
drink, first."

He flourished the bottle and the two soldiers, many a
fearful glance thrown behind, pushed and maneuvered
him around the corner of the building. Once out of sight,
they yielded to the Indian's generosity and each took a
stout peg from the proffered bottle. Perhaps, between
them, they lowered the quart by a scant three fingers. Big
Baby up-ended the returned container and emptied it
without taking a breath. Belching to show his fine man-
ners, he dropped the empty bottle into the dust, and
grinned, "Good stuff," and led the way on around to the
back of the store and in through the rear door.

Inside, the two troopers stood and gawked.

Crude, the arrangement was. And makeshift and odd-
like as only a horseback Indian's imagination would see
such a thing. But there was no mistaking the fact that
Milch's men's counter had been transformed into a ser-
viceable bar, presently stocked with more bottled-in-bond,
high-class drinking whiskey than either soldier had ever
seen in one place before. There was even a hawk-faced
Cheyenne brave with two braids and one feather slanted
across the rear of his head tending bar in a dude city suit
with black string tie, hardboiled shirt, pearl studs, and a
nosefull of gold cufflinks. And more! Two customers
leaned at the bar, already served. One looked like a Kan-

sas dirt farmer, the other a trailhand just in from Texas. But the atrocious bow of the legs and the turned-in toes of the beaded moccasins worn by both did not escape the astonished soldiers.

However, both men had been and seen the elephant before this. When in the land of Roman Nose, don't ask questions. With a nodding exchange of looks, the troopers moved to the bar. "Howdy, Tex," said one of them, to Dog Chips, and "Evening, Hiram," beamed the other upon Stick-of-Wood. "What are you drinking, gentlemen?" they chorused together, and "Whiskey," grunted the customers, as quickly. *"He-hau! He-hau!"*

The troopers had one, then had another one. Their money was worthless, Tex and Hiram standing treat insistently. The barkeep, too, was a man of golden heart, as well as noseplugs. When he poured, he poured. A drink was not a drink, it was a deluge. *"He-hau! He-*hic, *he-*hic, *he-*hic."

Shortly, Cross Feather signaled his two shills that the soldiers were sodden enough.

"Soldier-friends," the bartender announced, reaching over the bar and turning both fuddle-eyed clients to face the front door, "you go tell him other soldier-friend."

Steadied and aimed by Dog Chips and Stick-of-Wood, the troopers steered for the front of the store. There, the Indians pushed them out upon the boardwalk beneath the roofed porch, flung wide the doors of the emporium behind them. Within thirty-five seconds the rush was on.

A cavalryman can smell whiskey as far as his horse can scent water or sweet grass, and can run to find it as fast.

Presently Fat, who because of his white blood and hence greater resistance to temptation, had been given charge of the root-cellar supply room, had all that he could do to hand up the quarts of Old Crow to his perspiring comrades, Tex and Hiram. The discovery rush, kept quiet as possible by the troopers at first, for fear of officer disapproval, soon began to grow to a low hum, to a whining swarming-beehive noise, to a full-bore rumble of buffalo stampede.

The walls commenced to rock and stir upon their footings.

Upstairs, in his second-floor store building living quarters, Henry Milch came bolt upright on his bed, aroused from fitful and bedeviled sleep.

"My God!" he cried. "Tornado—!"

# 21

MESS HALL bound, Captain Strinker took a flanking route. He did not care to encounter any of his troops just then. He did so nevertheless.

Swinging by the kitchen latrine, he heard a scuffling which he attributed to rats. When this was augmented by heavy thumping from within, he merely muttered, "Big devils," and kept going. But when the thumps were overlain by human curses and muffled cries for succor, he came smartly about. "Who's in there?" he demanded.

Overwrought and not recognizing the voice of command, Fleeb, the shrewd one who had gotten them into the outhouse, stopped banging at the door, and dripped in tones honied with carbolic, "Just us two gorgeous blondes which have run away from Dodge City to seek our fortunes, soldier boy." To which Canister, the charmer of the pair, added, "Oh, yes, and my but it is cold in here with only these dancehall dresses on. Tee-hee!"

There was a moment of moonlit apoplexy on Strinker's part and Fleeb roared into it, "Well, for Christ's sake, you dogfaced dumb left-footed stable-swamper, let us out of here! What have we gotta do? Get a pass signed by that jackass Strinker? Come on, soldier, it ain't funny!"

The captain marched under rigid control to the door of

120

the weathered rest. There, he removed the pin which locked the hasp, still silent as a specter. Stepping back, he drew himself to his full five-feet-and-few-inches, and thundered magnificently, "You may come out, sirs—!"

The door flew open. And Strinker had misjudged its arc. It caught him up in its outward orbit and carried him with it, crushingly, into the wall planks of the little building. Fleeb and Canister, bombarding forth, failed at first to comprehend what had become of their benefactor. Then Canister giggled and said, "Tee-hee, Harry, he must of got swung inter the wall by the door," and Fleeb answered, "Marvin, you are a forty-carrot genius, that is percisely what's happent to the idiot," and both of them pulled the door away from the building to reveal the flattened officer.

The faces of the two soldiers at once grew paler than the moonlight. They stared in terror at what they had done. That wide black hat. That fringed buckskin shirt. The long yellow gauntlets. The famed red kerchief. It was impossible, yet there it was, and they had done it.

"*Jesus*," said Harry Fleeb, "*we've kilt General Custer.*"

And both troopers hit into a ramrod brace, holding it like two rocks, and wondering if they would be shot at sunrise or given life at hard labor.

## 22

THE WILD Cheyenne children, bivouacked in the supply annex of Kate Mehaffey's post kitchen, sat upon the earthen floor in a big-eyed circle. To represent the tribal camp fire, Red Dust, safely back from his journey to the jail, had placed a lantern on the dirt. And to calm the children so that they might soon go to the blankets which the powerful white woman had spread for them, the true nephew of Roman Nose had been telling them stories of the Cheyenne people, even as the village headmen had told those same stories about the fires of the winter camp along Sand Creek before the pony soldiers came.

"And so," the northern boy said, concluding the final tale of the night, "my uncle Maōx won that war with the fierce Absoroka, the thieving Crows. They had taken five ponies from my uncle. My uncle took back twenty-five ponies from them. And he also counted coup on fourteen of their best warriors, and his horse knocked over the lodge of the Crow chief and my uncle threw a rope around the lodgeskins, with the chief still inside of them, and he dragged the chief all the way to the river on the way home, and left him there in the water and that chief was ruined. No other Crow ever touched the forehead to him again. *Nohetto,* that is the end of the story."

One of the wild children scratched his head.

"You say your uncle's name is Maōx?" he asked. "That means 'Red Nose.' Why, then, is your uncle called Roman Nose?"

"The white man calls him that," replied Red Dust. "A mistake in the translation of his Cheyenne name."

"Oh. I like Red Nose better. It is nobler."

"Now," said another child, "if your uncle counted coup on fourteen Crows and stole back twenty-five horses, how is it that the news didn't get to our camp? Our village was up on the Platte that summer. We should have heard."

Red Dust arose haughtily.

"Do you deny the word of Roman Nose?" he demanded.

"Never!" protested the other boy. "But that's a lot of ponies."

"Yes," piped a third lad. "And dragging a chief inside his own tipi to the water? I don't know, Mahesie, maybe—"

"Enough!" stormed Red Dust. "Go to your blankets, all of you." He stared at them. "Miserable southern cubs!" he growled. "I wonder that Preacher bothered to put you in the wagon. All you want to hear are stories about sweet good spirits and happy times. Old women's tales, pah!"

Here, the lamplight from the kitchen intruded to end the exchange, as Mrs. Mehaffey opened the annex door to call for a bit of quiet. "Shure, now," she vowed, stabbing a sausage-finger at the shaggy-haired flock, "if yez don't simmer down, I'll come among yez wid me double-handled warclub." She brandished a flour-caked rolling pin, the children retreating with cries of, "*Momoxzéma-zistoz,* no, no, please, not that!" to the sanctuary of their makeshift pallets.

"Ah, dearies," soothed Kate, "'tis much better yez sound when spoke at wid a stick. Shure and I never belayved in being koind to dumbbrute animales. Spare the rod and spyle the Cheyenne, I always sed. Now, thin, yez dusky scuts; move wan inch off thim blankets and I'll cut yur hair clean down to yur eyebrows wid a blunt bone-saw, yez hear?

"Rid Dust." She wheeled on the northern boy. "Yez traipse along to the kitchen wid me. I may need yez fer a mayteerial witness whin thim darlin' slobs bust loose from the outhouse. I can hear thim now, a-starming into me premises wid the foul claim that I aided and a-butted yur excape, and that yez will have flew the coop, long since. Swayte Mary! whut a noight—and me Oirish spirits telling me it's scarce begun. Lah!"

She blew out the annex lantern, seized up the rope still trailing from Red Dust's neck. "Heel," she ordered, with an unmotherly tug upon the boy's leash, and marched back out into the kitchen, Red Dust dragging in her wake.

For a thoughtful moment the darkness in the annex went unbroken by sound, save the subdued breathing of the orphaned Washita children. Then a small girl spoke up, whisperingly.

"I think," she said, "that the Round Squaw could bring back more Crow hair than Roman Nose."

"Aye!" murmured a male child, admiringly. "And more ponies, too."

"Yes," sided a third youngster. "And if the ponies grew weary of carrying her, she could carry them. *Ih!*"

Since these things were unquestionably so, and as the children, like children the world around, responded with healthy enthusiasm to judicious force, the last speaker closed the forum for the evening, without dissent.

"I think," he said, "that we had all better cover our eyes and go to sleep. I don't want any haircut. Good night, dear friends."

124

"Yes, yes, good night."
"Maheo lead you."
"Happy visions, all of us."
"Yes, thank you."
"Good night."

BUCK PRIVATES, just reduced, Harry Fleeb and Marvin Canister marched stiffly into Mrs. Mehaffey's kitchen, the snout of Captain Strinker's big Colt revolver directing them from behind.

"Mrs. Mehaffey, these men claim that you have freed one of the Indian children, and locked them in the privy into the bargain. What have you to say?" Strinker made the charge, stood back waiting to have it confirmed. The Widow Mehaffey merely shook her head and gave a tug on the rope she held in her hand, and which disappeared beneath the kitchen table. Out slunk Red Dust and, taking the Indian view of the situation, began to bark at the intruders.

"Here, now, shut up, yez Cheyenne mongrel," commanded Kate. " 'Tis only the darlin' captain, with thim dear lads we seen drinking the whiskey whin they brung yez over here from the guardhouse. Smell their breaths, captain dearie, and loikwoise ask thim if this ain't the Injun tad they lift wid meself, whoiles they snuck out to swill that voil stuff."

Strinker glared, sampled the bourbon-laden breaths of the outmaneuvered soldiers, wheeled back to Kate.

"Mrs. Mehaffey, this command is in your debt," he ad-

126

mitted. "Will you kindly keep close watch of the Indian lad, until I can send a detail to return him to the guardhouse? Thank you, madam." He jabbed at the troopers with the big Colt. "March, you swine! One false move and you will be shot. Take the short way across the parade ground behind the sutler's store. Ho!"

Fleeb and Canister marched away, lock-stepping like tin soldiers. Perhaps en route to the jail, in some moonshadow, an opportunity would present itself. Escape was the only answer now. Short of going over the stockade and drawing twenty years for simple desertion, this night's work could win them life on the Dry Tortugas, or in the bake-hell pits of Fort Yuma. Hep, hep, hep . . .

Going toward the store Strinker's mind, too, was on the prowl of crimes and punishments. He could, in the clear light of the moon, see his career glimmering. Ten years in grade and now this. It was too much. If word of Bleek's rebellion leaked out of Fort Larking—ah, but why propose the worst? There was still hope; there was still Cumpston Funder. The boy would think of something; would come up with some way to re-barrel Bleek and his bad little Cheyenne apples.

The C.O. glanced toward Milch's place.

Curse it, that was the very devil of a racket the men were making over there by now. Nor did it sound as though it were any longer confined to the parade ground in front of the store. Indeed, the emporium was ablaze with lamplight. The celebration of Yellow Nose's war dance had spread inside, and was presently roaring full tilt.

"Liquor!" the captain cried out suddenly. "Dear Lord, those devils have somehow found whiskey!"

*What* whiskey? he instantly asked himself.

There was no strong drink on his post, save what the

surgeon had for medical needs at the hospital. And Dr. Hummerbund reliably prescribed every available drop of that scant supply for his own lamentable cholic, a condition which he described as having acquired in the Creek and Seminole Wars, and being similar to malaria tremens.

But where *had* the wicked stuff been hidden?

Bleek? Good Heavens, he was a known toper. Would it be possible that he peddled from his prairie schooner?

Stanley Schmerd had warned Strinker that the Preacher drank on the average of a barrel a month. Did he sell to the Indians and the isolated frontier garrisons to support his own habit?

There was no time for speculation, however.

The fact was that his men—Strinker's own command— were out of hand and shouting drunk in the post store. Action must be taken. The command must be re-seized, then pressed to its ultimate. Funder had failed, clearly. All that remained of hope for Fort Larking rode with the iron will and fighting heart, loath to arouse, but a fury incredible once fired, of Captain Julius Caesar Strinker, Commanding.

"Men," he said, voice firm, quiet, steely; "you are still under charge and arrest, but your duty lies with mine. You, Fleeb, and you, Canister, are cavalrymen. Your captain asks that you follow him. Forward, ho—!"

The troopers looked at one another and shrugged. All right, the C.O. had finally worked loose his headstall. If it made him happy, seeing that he held the gun and that it was cocked, and he was cracked, why, fine, Fleeb and Canister were not going to argue any orders.

"Yes sir," they saluted, and started on.

Angling across the rear yard of the store, they ran upon the parked Argonaut. Veering to detour it, they heard the faint cry for help which drifted from its silvered canvas top and, glancing up, beheld Second Lieutenant Cump-ston Funder astride the midstays and signaling frantically to them of some danger unseen. Strinker, thinking his aide had broken down in command, herded Fleeb and Canister back toward the wagon, ignoring the lieutenant's urgent hand signals to go back, or rather, to stay back away from the parked vehicle. When he saw that his superior would not heed, Funder hoarsely shouted, *sotto voce,* for Strin-ker to take note of the large and very hairy Cheyenne wolf dog which squatted guard at the Argonaut's off-front wheel, the remnants of Funder's breeches pendent from his jaws.

But Julius Strinker was fighting again now.

This was the old "Deathwind Strinker" of Cemetery Ridge, Chickamauga, the Hornet's Nest, and Bloody Pond, before the fragment of grape struck low the captain courageous, and invalided him out to the frontier.

"Men," he commanded Fleeb and Canister, "take that brute in hand and leash him to the vehicle. Lieutenant Funder, sir, get down from that ridiculous perch immedi-ately. And where are your pants, man?"

"The dog has them, sir," replied Funder. "And begging your pardon, Captain, I will stay here until the animal is picketed. He's dragging a chain, sir, and—"

At this point, Lame Wolf emerged from the moon shadow which had been hiding him where he crouched by the flanks of the Kiowa mares, waiting for Funder to fall asleep before he did and, hopefully, to slide off the wagon top.

For the first time Strinker and his two jailbirds saw the nature of the enemy.

The captain paled, but whipped out his saber.

Fleeb and Canister shared one common gurgle of ter-ror, and took off for the stockade. Lame Wolf uttered his killing roar and went after them. The last Strinker saw of the disgraceful rout, the fleeing troopers were scaling the ten-foot logs, the great wolf-brute ravening at their boot-soles. With total disgust, the Captain whirled away from this shame to face the other: Lieutenant Funder in his underwear.

"Sir," he shouted up, "get down at once from that wagon, and cover yourself!"

Funder, thinking Lame Wolf to be still gnawing at the stockade, commenced to descend. He had reached a precarious position of one foot on the driver's box, the other spread-eagled to reach the off-wheel hub, when the Cheyenne dog came snarling back on duty. Cumpston Funder seemed not to scramble back astride the Argonaut so much as to vault-to-seat without visible means of mounting.

Strinker understood then that he had come to another of the combat officer trials-by-enemy-fire.

"Funder," he ordered, "keep calm, sir; I shall confine the animal myself."

The lieutenant recoiled in horror.

"No, no, not that!" he cried down in desperation, but was too late.

Strinker had committed himself.

He had actually reached for Lame Wolf's chain.

The unwitting nerve of this act was suicidal, but at the same time its very cheek saved Strinker's life. Lame Wolf, leaping for the officer's throat, missed his target as the captain stooped to take up the loose end of the dog's chain. The great brute sailed on over the reprieved C.O. and, his timing thrown off by the unexpected miss of the prey, landed awkwardly. His momentary disorientation permitted Funder to stretch down to his superior the hand of salvation.

Strinker, shaken by the vision of the wolf dog's snarling launch at his jugular vein, seized the proffered hand and was hauled to the wagon's top just as Lame Wolf recovered and churned back to the attack.

As it was, the post commandant lost a portion of his uniform in the escape. Even as Funder before him, he left upon the field, in the jaws of the enemy, the lower half of his General Custer outfit. As well, he lost the entire trapdoor to the long winter underwear which he wore beneath the yellow-striped leggins.

His saviour, staring now in some dismay, not unmixed however with a healthy curiosity, at the exposed gluteus of Captain Julius Caesar Strinker, saluted his leader.

"Why, Captain," he said, squinting down to where Strinker lay, bottom-up, across his lap, "you never told me that charge of grapeshot at Chickamauga took you in the—"

"Funder, you fool! Shut up—*BaaaaawwwWWWW-----!*"

With the aborted command, Captain Strinker began to beat in anguish with his clenched fists upon the canvas top of the Argonaut, and to kick and squall in broken tantrum, while the hot tears flowed like funneled salt.

# 24

IN THE dizzying heat of Cell One, the two forms on the rammed earth floor stirred with feeble life. In his efforts to be fair, not wanting either unconscious man to catch cold, Preacher had re-stoked the already glowing stove before departing with the children. Also, for the same humanitarian reason, he had liberally anointed the sleepers with whiskey. Might they not require a restorative aromatic upon awakening? Of course. Now if Funder or Strinker, returning to discover the lads in drunken stupor upon the floor of Preacher's cell, and Preacher, with his dusky birds, long flown—if either officer, that is, then wanted to believe that Edward or Stanley had been drinking on duty, well, what could an honest missionary from Horse Creek do about that?

Thus it was that returning conscience, not to be confused with consciousness, which was also obtaining, brought to the pair on the dirt floor a certain, if somewhat fuzzy, revelation of their entrapment.

"God help us!" cried Schmerd, first to recover and note the empty cells. "He's gone and he's took the kids!"

"Yes," said faithful Blemmish, shaking his head and hearing faint and beautiful chimes still ringing in his ears. "And he has spilled whiskey all over us, and if—"

132

"Jeez!" interrupted the sergeant. "That's so! We'll both get busted back to buck private, maybe even executed or, worse yet, shipped back east into combat. We mustn't let Funder or Strinker find us here!"

Leaping to his feet, he raced for the cell door.

"You hide your own self," he yelled to Blemmish. "Me, I'm going to throw myself on Kate's mercy. Maybe she'll let me use her root cellar. Maybe she'll desert with me and we can make a run for Mexico."

"Stanley, wait—!" Blemmish's plea was stirred by a sudden thought that his friend of the years in service was still too groggy to know his true way. For one very vital consideration, he did not appear to realize that he was out of uniform. But the corporal's cry came too late. Schmerd was already down the corridor and out the front door of the guardhouse, kitchen-bound across the moon-patched parade ground.

With a groan the loyal Blemmish staggered to his feet and set out after Schmerd. The sergeant was not built for speed. With luck, the corporal might catch up to him before some commissioned officer did.

But the fickle jade smiled not.

Nearing Milch's store, Blemmish had not closed the gap on galloping Stanley. And, passing near the rear of the establishment, the gallant corporal was hailed by the clarion voice of command.

"Blemmish, you fool! Stop chasing that damned Indian, and give us a hand here!"

Skidding to a halt, while Stanley galloped on to disappear in a cloud of moondust toward Kate's kitchen, Blemmish struck a brace and saluted the two officers on top of the parked prairie schooner.

"Yes sir, Captain," he answered. "What'd you have in mind, sir?"

"This dog. This miserable cur. He has us treed."

Blemmish peered hard toward the head of the wagon. "Yes sir," he saluted again. "He surely has, that's a fact, sir."

"You idiot!" Strinker's screech was subdued but penetrating. "Grab his chain and hook him to the rear of the wagon, do you hear?"

By this time the uproar from the Cheyenne Bar of Milch's store was deafening. The corporal had to shout with cupped hands to make his reply heard.

"Yes, sir. I hear, all right. That ain't the problem."

For his part, Strinker now realized that the need for holding down voices for fear of discovery by some enlisted personnel was long since drowned by the tumult and sodden singing coming from the emporium. Not only was there no chance of being overheard above the pandemonium, but any troopers who might totter by would be so saturated they wouldn't know a captain from a corporal, even without his pants on. "All right, Blemmish," he bellowed back—squawked, really. "What's your trouble?"

"My feet, sir. They won't move toward that dog."

"Blemmish! !"

"Yes sir, Captain?"

"This is an order—collar that damned dog!"

The corporal considered his options. If he obeyed and were successful in tethering the hairy cur, he might be let off with demotion and loss of pay with rank. If he disobeyed, following Schmerd over the wall with Mrs. Mehaffey, the firing squad awaited recapture. And the Rio Grande was one terribly long walk from Fort Larking.

"Sir," said Edward A. Blemmish, "I am going to try it."

Lieutenant Funder, silent until now, brightened.

"Good lad!" he called, meaning to build moral support

for the dangerous mission. "Is the next of kin current on your papers?"

"Funder—!" screeched Strinker in fury.

But, as with the captain in his turn, it was too late to salvage all of Corporal Blemmish, Edward A.

He lost both brogans to Lame Wolf and bore upward with him to the wagon top only his life, his fortune, and his sacred honor.

# 25

HENRY MILCH bounded from bed. In old-fashioned night-shirt and tasseled cap he was not the picture to inspire timidity or doubt in the criminal breast. Realizing this, Milch paused to arm himself with a pepperbox derringer from a dresser drawer, before plunging into the outer hallway. Whoever or whatever was raising all that hell downstairs in his store had best beware. Henry Milch, by nature not a fighter, had had about all that he needed of spurring that day. If those wastrel rowdies of Strinker's command thought they could invade private property simply because a state of siege had suspended business—well! they didn't know Henry Milch; much less his connections in Washington, D.C.

But once down the length of the unlighted hallway, and poised upon the upper landing of the stairway which went downward into the rear of store—the stairway which terminated behind Ladies' Wear and Better Linens —Milch lost momentum.

He lost it very suddenly.

In truth, he dove for the landing floor behind the carved palings of the stairway's rail, and clung there pale as rigor mortis rewarmed.

My God! Was he dreaming? Was this some nightmare

of the middle mind? Some fantasy of an overwrought *systema nervus?* Or was it all for hard and bitter fact? *Were* those Fort Larking troopers staggering drunkenly all over the store? *Was* that a facsimile saloon fashioned of his hardware counter and trophy moosehead, and his $500 French looking glass? Lord have mercy on his tottering reason, *were* those Smoky Hill Cheyenne warriors serving up the liquor to the soldiers? And, chimera of all chimeras! was that his hidden and sequestered illicit bonded bar whiskey being peddled from the root cellar to the hardware section by that fat waddling Cheyenne in the checkered kitchen apron and polka-dotted emigrant-woman's sunbonnet?

'Fore God, it *was!*

Milch knew the smell of bonded bourbon.

It owned no honest kinship with the formaldehyde-and-fusel-oil odor of frontier trade whiskey.

He was being robbed blind. And worse. He was vulnerable to exposure of his smuggling trade, with consequent ruin and legal involvement from which not even his friends in Washington might preserve him. What must be done?

Well, in doubt, always call out the military.

It had been a Milch commercial tradition for two generations of frontier retail rapine to camp-follow the army. This alliance made friends who would rattle the saber to drum up or, in emergencies such as this, to defend business. Also, there was the matter of property, simple physical real estate, to consider. And that was a Constitutional right, guaranteed in writing by the founding fathers! At the thought, Milch's breast swelled, his pulses hammered. Down the stairway, there, those devils were depriving him of his Constitutional guarantees. They were devastating not only his civil but also his capitalistic rights.

And more! Was there not also in the famed document something about the sanctity of privacy? You were damned right there was. Those soldiers were invading his privacy, as well as tearing down his store and despoiling his stock-in-trade.

The animals!

This was the classic mob. Rioting. Looting. Boozing.

They would be wenching, too, were there any assaultable female within a hundred miles.

Brutes, brawlers, traitors, revolutionaries!

As these higher inspirations invaded the brain and bloodstream of Henry Milch, he was rising from the floor, wheeling down the hallway, back past his room and to the window at the end of the hall and rear of the building.

Flinging up the sash, he leaned far out, his hands straining at the grip of the sill, neck veins standing forth to signal the pressure of his trumpet call for freedom.

"Help! Murder! Arson! Treason! Get the guards! Strinker, you idiot, call out the guards! Somebody do something! These bloody troops—Funder! Strinker! Schmerd! Blemmish! Anybody!—your damned troops are gutting my store. They've broken into my booze. They're selling it to the Indians. No, wait, it's the Indians who are selling it to them. Help! Help! Military police—!"

"Milch, you confounded fool!" The high scratchy voice interrupted to hail the storekeeper from below. "Stop that caterwauling and throw us down a rope!"

"Police! Guards! Call out the—what the devil is that down there? Is that you, Strinker? What are you doing on top of that damned wagon?"

"I might ask you what you're doing in that damned window in your nightshirt and cap, as well, you infernal merchant. Do as I say. Throw us down something to climb up with."

"The devil I will. Get down from there your own way,

and go and bring those rioting troops under control this instant, or your commission will be lifted with the first telegraph communication east." Milch leaned farther out, peering down. "Good Lord, is that you, too, Cumpston? I thought you, at least, had better sense."

"Perhaps I did, Mr. Milch," said the young lieutenant "But I was outranked. Be a good fellow, like the Captain says, sir, and throw us down a climbing line."

"Blast it, Funder! Why don't you and that dunderhead C.O. get down off that silly wagon top and take charge of that outrage downstairs in my store? Why must I haul you up here?"

From the star-crossed top of the Argonaut, a third cavalry voice interceded plaintively. "Well, you see, sir," called up Corporal Blemmish, "the truth is that the Captain and the Lieutenant got themselves treed by this here mean and spiteful Injun wild dog, and got the crotches chewed out of their—OUCH!—now why did you go and do that for, Captain? You know it's agin regulations for a officer to strike a enlisted man."

"What the corporal means," shouted Strinker desperately, "is that we cannot very well resume command until we repair our uniforms. Now get a line down here, Milch, or I shall blow your insipid brains out from between your ears!"

Strinker actually made the motions of drawing, cocking, and leveling to dead-bead his Colt .45 cavalry revolver on the proprietor above. But here Blemmish reached out and touched his pointing arm respectfully.

"Sir," he said, "ain't you forgetting that the dog done grabbed your pistol and belt along with your pants, sir?"

Strinker looked at the aimed hand. He pulled its curled trigger finger on the emptiness of the night air, then shook his head in somewhat puzzled chagrin.

"Well," he temporized upward, "don't just stand there

in that dratted window staring at me, Milch. Move out!"

Milch retreated to his bedroom and returned with some knotted sheets by which the treed cavalrymen began the climb to the window and the momentary safety of the upper hallway. An unsympathetic fate, however, caught them in the act of escape. While the trio was yet but half the distance to the window, shorn backsides glistening in the moonlight, around the corner of the building marched Preacher Bleek and his orphans of the Arkansas.

"*Zetōoxtoz,* Preacher!" cried Blackbird, pointing in amazement. "Look there! Three pony soldiers going up a wall without any pants on!"

"Indeed," nodded Preacher, halting to peer. "A miracle. The Lord God Jehovah has smote their minds."

Sunflower tugged at his great hand.

"No," corrected the little Arapaho girl. "It is Lame Wolf, and he has smote their behinds."

Preacher looked down at her. "Ah," he said softly. Then, as Strinker, Funder and Blemmish vanished, drop-seats up, through the second-story window, he murmured to the tiny Indian girl, "You be my true small love, Sunflower, and as right as rain puddles in the dust."

He swept the lame child into his arms, sat her upon one broad shoulder, turned in booming cheer to the others.

"Come!" he said, gesturing toward the Argonaut. "Let the Lord's work be did. What Lame Wolf has put together, let no pony soldier put asunder. Glory, glory!"

"Amen! Amen!" cried Blackbird.

And his comrade, Buzzard, surveying the field, and all the demented people upon it, added with solemn wisdom, "Jesus help us."

140

## 26

YELLOW NOSE understood that the moment of the charge was at-hand. He could feel the power of the medicine working within him. He knew that Maheo would protect him. No pony soldier lead might touch him. No whirling blade of the longknives, the bayonets, would cut his skin. His war-powers had come to him, at last.

Moreover, it was getting cold in the dance hole.

His fire had gone out and for the past hour no good friendly trooper had come to hand him down kind words and a bit of dry wood. In fact, the troopers had all disappeared. He could hear the noise of their singing, but it was muffled and Yellow Nose knew the dread feeling of the mummer whose audience has walked out on him.

Well, so be it. If those dolts could not remember how near to final destruction they were, Heovese, the yellow-beaked Ute hawk of the northern Cheyenne, would not warn them again. It would be easier to take them from the rear, as they wandered off, anyway. Hah! the fools.

Yellow Nose went into the final glassy-eyed rigidity of the warrior prepared to die, should the red gods fail him or his medicine weaken.

Three more times went he around the cold ashes of the fire, gathering momentum.

141

Away sailed the eaglebone flute.

Discarded were his leggins and all other accouterments of the outer body. The Cheyenne went naked into war, that no foreign body of his own bearing might be driven by lance or bullet into his flesh, so bringing infection and death. At the end of the third lap of the sudden sprinting and disrobing about the perimeter of the cooling ambers, the small but incredibly fierce adopted son of Spotted Wolf threw back his head, uttered the blood-chilling wolf cry of the northern hostiles, and charged the retreating rears of the cowardly pony soldiers.

It was a short charge.

With skull-bending force, Yellow Nose brought up against the earthen sides of the hole he had dug for himself with his nine-hour dance in the middle of the post road in front of Henry Milch's trading store.

In the terminal frenzy and glory of the working of his personal medicine for war, he had forgotten that he had passed below the surface some time after sundown.

Now, clad only in breech-clout and courage, he was knocked backward into the ash-covered coals of his fire.

There he sat shaking his vibrating head, until the not-so-dead coals ignited the string of his clout, at which signal a phenomenon of western Kansas folklore, still recounted on reservation and in pioneer home, took place.

Yellow Nose had forgotten to remove one item of personal equipment in preparing for his charge. This was his powderhorn which, since he had no gun to go with it, the kindly troopers had permitted him to keep for his dance.

Now, in the jarring impact with the dirt of the hole's wall, the plug of this container had been dislodged and the contents of the horn spilled into the front pouch of the little warrior's gee-string. When, with half a pound of #3 DuPont Black Riflepowder lodged in the forepart of the

142

clout, the rearstring of the garment took fire from the smoldering coals of the dance pit, the legend was launched—along with Yellow Nose.

Two drunken soldiers staggering out upon the boardwalk in front of Milch's store to get a breath of air drew back in befuddled wonder and drinkstruck awe. Up out of the post roadway before their very eyes burst a tremendous belching fireball with a thunderous explosion. Skyward streamed the ball of flame, showering ten thousand sparks, bearing aloft one small Indian chief, in an arc which carried from the roadway high over the stockade-top and flaring downward out of sight into the maw of the moonlit prairie, beyond.

"Gawd!" mumbled one of the troopers. "J'ever see a shooting star bounce like that? We could've been kilt!"

And so was born the folk-myth of Heovese's Comet.

# 27

SAFELY BEHIND the locked door of Henry Milch's bedroom, the military staff took council with the civilian management of Fort Larking. The burden of the conference was the avenues of undetected escape from the store's second-story quarters. To this tactical problem Milch, apparently, had a happy solution. There was an outside stairway on the far side of the building—the dark side. "Splendid," said Strinker, drawing tight about his flanks the borrowed blanket, whose bedmate shrouded the hams of Lieutenant Cumpston Funder. "Follow me, men."

The others, recognizing the flint-and-steel of command when it struck them with its fiery sparks, fell in behind the fearless captain. The hallway door to the outside stairway was gained without incident. But all realized, from the ever-increasing uproar down in the store, that it would be only a matter of moments before some of the revelers commenced prowling the upper regions of Milch's emporium. Strinker, however, was cool as camphorated corn-vanisher.

"All right," he ordered, low-voiced. "Single file and no smoking in the ranks."

Out they went upon the moonwashed landing—Strinker first, then Funder and Milch, still in his nightshirt and cap, with Corporal Blemmish, least damaged of uniform or morale, bringing up the rear.

They got nearly halfway down the outer stairs before Santiago, stationed on scout by Preacher, caught the refraction of the moonrays from the captain's alabaster shanks. "*Mira*, Preacher!" cried the Mexican-Apache waif, and the probe of the perimeter was contained.

"Hi!" shouted the Horse Creek man, unchaining the just re-chained Lame Wolf. "Go get 'em, *Enònika!*"

Responding to command and to the use of his Cheyenne familiar name, "Lame One," the long-furred brute roared full charge toward the outer staircase. Blemmish was knocked flat and stampeded by three separate retreats, *boomp! boomp! boomp!* as first Milch, then Funder, then Strinker wheeled by-the-right-flank and ran over him, bound for the upper hallway door in panic reverse.

In fact, the poor corporal, just staggering up from the third decking, was struck by a fourth, even greater force. Lame Wolf, yellow burning eye fastened on the main game, never seemed to see the measly noncom, but ran over him with the same disdain as Milch & Company, hot to bring down a captain or a lieutenant or, at least, a post sutler, to drag back to show Preacher what a good dog he was. By this devotion, Blemmish was spared a fate worse than losing the back half of his pants. Never the kind to deprecate small favors, the corporal slid on down the stairs behind Lame Wolf. Whirling about, he fled along the dark wall of the building to disappear into the parade ground shadows toward the post mess hall, along the moccasin tracks of his departed comrade-in-arms, Sergeant Stanley Schmerd, ghost war chief of the Smoky Hill Cheyenne.

He ran hard, and he ran well.

But he was still far, far too late to save his friend.

## 28

STANLEY SCHMERD raced through the night. Ahead loomed the post kitchens, with the lamp-of-love set in the steaming window to guide the distant traveler. But, wait. No. That was not the welcome shine of Wee Katie's kitchen lamp. It was only the glaring of the moon off-angled to the well-scrubbed panes. Damn! this was foul luck, to find the widow so early to bed. Well, she would simply have to be routed out. Her moment's frenzied flirtation with Preacher Bleek aside, Stanley knew that her true heart beat for him; and he was in clear and present danger.

"Ho, Kate!" he called, scratching at the lunared panes. "It's me, your very own Stanley. Psst! Psst!"

He held, one foot upraised, listening.

Nothing.

If she was indeed to bed so soon, Mrs. Mehaffey snored on. Schmerd pressed his bulbous snout to the window, shading out the moon with cupped hands. In the kitchen's dim light, he saw only emptiness. Tiptoeing lightly as some hamstrung moose, he came to the annex where the wild children slept. A moonbeam let him see, through that window, the peaceful faces of the dark-skinned orphans in repose. If one of those dusky faces were not so peaceful, it was only the luck of the night for Stanley Schmerd. If, in

146

its corner pool of the room's blackness, that alien face watched the hulking sergeant with other thought than that he was the war-painted Cheyenne brave his furnishings made him seem, the features gave no sign. And if, when Stanley had tiptoed on toward Wee Katie's boudoir pane, the owner of that wakeful face slid quickly out of the annex to reach the Round White Squaw ahead of him, charge what followed to the bill of Preacher Bleek: Red Dust was but a simple Indian lad from Old Wyoming; what comprehension he, of the strange games played by the pony soldier sergeant?

Kate Mehaffey came upright upon her cot, the slim hand of the red youth pressed in warning to her lips.

"Get up, Round Squaw," the northern boy whispered. "A bad one stalks outside."

No sooner had the words caused Kate's fat heart to skip a beat than the moon was blotted from her bedroom window.

"Jayzus save us!" she announced. "A Injun payping Tom!"

"Him hostile," murmured the northern boy. "Face paint black, yellow. Get gun."

The widow Mehaffey was of fighting stock. She paled a trace but hesitated not. Adorned as clad for bed, a vision from some nether lair of femininity, she swept into the kitchen, seized a shotgun from the dusty pegs above the woodbox.

Frizzled orange hair stood out from her head in curlers made from shucks of corn shellacked in place by starch-paste. A flowing robe of horsefeed-sacking and bedsocks fashioned of fringed yellow cavalry gauntlets sewed onto feet of U.S. saddlepad felting clad her for the encounter. Her dimpled chin, cow-broad jowls, and freckle-spattered brow were beauty-creamed with her own Fort Larking emollient mix of gunbore grease and gopher fat, equal parts with harness soap and paris green. Nor did she quail, now, as her hand tightened on the double trigger and door-latch.

Outside, Schmerd came skulk-a-toeing along the wall. Thwarted at annex and boudoir, it was in his fertile mind to jacknife-pick the kitchen lock, a trysting wile well-tried err this.

But Kate, never wondering how the Cheyenne night-crawling hostile brave might know of Stanley's knifeblade pass, threw wide the door the instant that the lock was scraped; threw wide the door and hipped the old twelve-gauge with a Killarney war cry of her own.

Stanley Schmerd recoiled in honest terror, a strangled scream of naked fear in his throat.

God in Heaven, what creature from the Pit was this, which had so plainly invaded Kate's domain, and no doubt gobbled all who slept therein, or cut the common throat?

Away wheeled Schmerd, no thought for Big Baby's clothing which he wore, or facepaint which gleamed so brightly in the moon, or warrior's bristling roach of ponied hair barbered during drunken sleep by Preacher Bleek.

As for Kate, great arms akimbo in the doorway, fat fingers yet clenched in the clutch of doom upon the shotgun's two set-triggers, she saw only the fleeing rear of a bloodthirsty hostile warrior.

Too late the shrill-cried echo of Edward Blemmish's pleas to "wait! wait!"—that it was only Stanley Schmerd who galloped there in Smoky Hill accouterment.

The little corporal dashed up in panting time to duck for earth and save his own white hide, as over him roared the old smoothbore, and through the night toward the

148

rear of Sergeant Schmerd whizzed double charges of #00 buckshot.

Schmerd, though struck with both barrels, full and modified, gave but a single one great cry, and plunged to earth a broken and a bloodied thing. From the doorway Kate Mehaffey, breaking weapon and blowing smoke calmly from the breech through both grimed bores, called out to know what she had downed—unknown brave, or chief of high renown—and was rewarded with a screech from loyal Blemmish which curdled even Katie's Irish nerve.

" 'Fore Gawd!" wept the little corporal, heartwrenchingly and bawled for all the night to hear. "You'll swing for this, you Ball of Fat! you've killed my dear friend, Stanley—!"

But Kate was made of Irish wool, and more than a yard of it wide. Swinging broad face to shining moon, she nodded up to where all good Irish sergeants go, and crossed herself with simple dignity.

"Ah, Dinnis, lad," she sighed, "did not I say I'd git the murthering scut whut drilled yez? Faith, now, me boy; yez can slaype azey up thir: ye're even."

Coming about to go back into her kitchen, the beamy widow was confronted by Red Dust, standing all the while behind her. The Indian boy nodded somberly.

"Maybeso him sleep good up there," he said, pointing starward. "But you no sleep good down here."

"Whut the divil do yez mean, yez red whelp?"

"You killum pony soldier sergeant. Pretty quick him come get you other pony soldier. Put long rope you likum halter, and throw other end over gateway, then haul 'em up likum—"

"Ah, that's enough, yez rascal," said Kate, giving him a shove into the kitchen. "Go and get yur little red frinds.

149

Shure and it's toime to change me luck, and me residence. Yez all may as well tag along wid old Kate."

Red Dust shook his head.

"Heap wrong," he said. "You come us. We all go home with preacher."

Kate Mehaffey stared at the Indian boy a moment, blue eyes shining. "Bejabbers!" she said. "Out of the mouths of babes!" And, sweeping up Red Dust like a sack of kitchen flour, went on a lumbering lope for the annex.

# 29

THE TWO besotted troopers who had witnessed the orbiting of Yellow Nose decided to return to the store and recount the adventure. They found few among their own number ready to listen to tales of Cheyenne fireballs. However, when, in desperation, they repeated the sighting of the phenomenon to the bartender, Cross Feather, the Indian leaned over the counter to his two nearest Cheyenne shills, Dog Chips and Big Baby.

"Friends," he said, "we have been selfish, small of thought. These two pony soldiers claim that Yellow Nose has disappeared. Go at once and see. Follow his trail, and tell him we are sorry that we forgot to bring him out some whiskey. Tell him to come back—the drinks are on the tipi."

Dog Chips growled some oath and slunk for the door. His ward Big Baby trotted in his wake. Both weaved a bit along the way. In moments, they were leaning over peering into the empty dance pit. "Hello, down there," called Dog Chips. "Are you down there, Heovese?" There was no reply, and Big Baby boomed, "Ho, speak up, no tricks, or we will drown you out!" He made a gesture to implement the threat with nature's weapon, but his guardian slapped his hands and told him that he was a bad boy and must not think of such mean child's play at serious moments. "Listen," he admonished, "something is very wrong here. See all that charred earth about the edges of the hole? Smell that acrid lingering of powder smoke? Curse them, the devils; the pony soldiers have blown him out of his hole to save the fort from his attack." Big Baby covered his mouth with both slab-paws, a look of horror upon his honestly murderous face. "What a wicked and cruel thing to do!" he cried. "Come, friend Dog Chips. We must tell this to Cross Feather, and all then make a war on the white soldiers. Not only will they be easy to kill while they are so robbed of their good brains by the *vèhoemàp*, but there will be all the more *vèhoemàp* left for us!"

Dog Chips showed his yellowed canines in appreciation of the thought, but shook his head.

"There's plenty of whiskey," he said. "No danger of running out. And why worry old Cross Feather about this? Let's just tell him Yellow Nose's medicine went cold and he crawled up out of the hole and went home."

"Oh, no," shuddered Big Baby. "That would be a lie. It's a wrong thing to tell a lie."

"You great sheephead, you!" Dog Chips glared at him. "How do you know it's a lie? Do you know his medicine did not go cold? That he did not crawl up out of the hole? That he did not go home? Bah! What's a lie? Only something you get caught telling. If they don't learn anything to the contrary, then no untruth has been stated. Back to the *vèhoemàp*. Somebody may be drinking up our share!"

"A tragic thing!" agreed Big Baby. "And true."

Both braves staggered up onto the boardwalk and into the store. At the bar, Cross Feather asked about Yellow Nose. "Oh," replied Big Baby, "he got weak in his hole and took some cold medicine and—" Dog Chips kicked

152

him in the shins with all his might and, when he yowled and bent over to grab the injured legbone, struck him in the back of his pony soldier sergeant's hat with an empty whiskey bottle. Big Baby went to his hands and knees and began crawling around in circles on the floor complaining that the last drink was too strong and that he would like a little water in the next one. Dog Chips, ignoring him, told Cross Feather that Yellow Nose had given up the idea of attacking Fort Larking and hit out for the Smoky Hill.

"Well, here," said Cross Feather, breaking the neck off a new bottle of Old Crow, and handing the bottle over the counter to Dog Chips. "Have his drink for him, and kindly go and tell Fat that we need some more *vèhoemàp* to be brought up from the little cave, right away."

Dog Chips stepped over the floor-wandering Big Baby, started toward the root cellar. But, along the way, he encountered a charming creature robed in white settler woman's sunbonnet and silver-buckled black shiny shoes tripping demurely between forms of reveling soldiers clogging her path toward the bar. The enchanting one bore a burden of some several bulky shapes bound up within an apron tied at her shapely waist, the necessary raising of the same garment exposing limbs and vistas of the bearer which, in the store's smoky light, Dog Chips imagined to be female. Alas, when he made his veering clutch to snare the winsome lass before some thieving white trooper might do so, he realized too late that what he had encompassed was not of the weaker sex.

"You crazy drunken Indian!" raged Fat, and dropping his upraised apron and all the bottles of whiskey cradled within it, he drew his tomahawk and bounced its rawhide-covered head of flintstone two times upon the low forehead of Dog Chips. The latter went to all fours without a murmur, and commenced to crawl. Very soon he met a friend peering at him from between the legs of a swaying cavalryman who had mounted that friend for the long journey across the floor to the bar.

"Why, hello, there," smile Big Baby. "Where have you been, Dog Chips, dear comrade? We are playing horse. Do you want to play, too?"

"No," snarled the other, "I'm a dog!" And drawing back, he ran at the leg of Big Baby's rider. Big Baby reared up in fright, but the cavalryman retained his seat and put the spurs into the huge Indian. Big Baby neighed, kicked, took off on the gallop, Dog Chips barking furiously at his heels.

As they went by the bar for the first time, scattering patrons in every direction, Cross Feather leaned out over the counter and, watching them disappear into the crowd, nodded to Fat who had just come up with the regathered apron-load of Old Crow, and suggested that the time had come to close up for the night.

Fat, surveying the situation, agreed.

"We will just start them on this new load I have here," he said, "and go."

"You know something," nodded Cross Feather, "business has been so heavy, I haven't had time for a drink myself."

"Precisely my situation, as well," said Fat. He reached for two of the bottles, while Cross Feather secured and slid down the counter to him a pair of one-pint beer mugs. Catching the mugs, Fat drew an ancient Colt from beneath his apron and shot the necks off two bottles of Old Crow, pouring from the two bottles into the two mugs simultaneously. Brimming the mugs, he sat the bottles upon the bar with twin loud thumps, and he and Cross

154

Feather swept up their overflowing mugs, clinking them soundingly.

"Here's *hau*," they grunted.

And the two braves tilted their mugs and drank them empty.

# 30

UPSTAIRS IN the living quarters of proprietor Milch, staff council had resumed. This time, with Lame Wolf guarding the parapet of the outside stairway landing and Corporal Blemmish either killed or missing in action, the options for a military breakthrough were severely reduced. They had indeed been boiled down to one supremely risky route, the mere envisioning of which would have made Tamerlane take pause.

"We have got to do it," Strinker was saying. "There is no other way than through the store itself; and if I do not get out of here and into fresh uniform, God knows where the night will lead us all."

"It will lead you to Fort Leavenworth jail, if I have my way!" raged the sutler. "And as for you, Funder, you jackanapes, when I get through talking to my connections in the Capitol, you will be lucky to be a buck private!"

"Oh, dear, oh, dear," said Funder, wringing his hands.

"Chin up, Cumpston," ordered Strinker. "Our friend the proprietor, here, is forgetting that the Cheyenne have uncovered his little cache. I think Milch, that being reasonable, being at the very least conservative, a Federal court will be unusual which will not hand you twenty years at hard labor. In any event, I would suggest that we all string together, or we shall all—"

"I believe you will find, sir," interrupted Funder, "that the correct quote is, 'we must all hang together, or we shall all surely hang separately.' Something to do with the American Revolution, sir. Very famous."

"Thank you, Cumpston," squeaked Strinker. "You bloody fool!"

"Good God," said Milch, cupping an ear to the sounds downstairs. "Listen to that. Something has happened."

It seemed true. The high buzz of anger had been added to the harmony of the reveling swarm.

"If a fight starts," whispered Funder, "we'll never get out. We'll be trapped by refugees, found out, revealed, ruined."

"Shut up," commanded Strinker. "I must think."

"While you're thinking," replied the lieutenant, "think about the fact that Bleek and the orphans are loose."

"Yes," snapped Milch. "Loose, and preparing to flee in that cursed old wagon. If they get away now, if they manage to escape Fort Larking and find that troublemaker Kindthorpe, we'll have the Indian Bureau *and* the Army to deal with. You must do something, Strinker."

"Ah!" cried the captain, "I have it. Funder."

"Yes, sir."

"Make a scout—make two scouts—first to the landing overlooking the store. See what those rascals are getting ugly about down there. Then go to the rear window and determine what Bleek is up to. See if the wagon is still there, what the Preacher is doing—everything."

"And then?" asked Funder.

"Return at once, if you can, and we will take it from there."

"Take what from where?" demanded Milch. "Strinker,

you are an absolute ass. Sending this nincompoop to look out the back window or spy on those criminals down below is not my idea of doing something. I meant *we* have got to do something, you fatuous moron!"

Strinker drew himself up. Even if naked of nether limb, he still had on his fringed buckskin shirt, elbow yellow gauntlets, red neckcloth, and black Custer hat.

"No commander can move without adequate information," he said coldly. "Lieutenant Funder, please advance."

Funder saluted and left the room. It seemed to the two awaiting his return that he had scarcely closed the door before he was back.

"Sir," he said, saluting smartly. "Second Lieutenant Cumpston Clark Funder, sir, reporting results of—"

"Funder!!"

"Yes, sir. Well, you won't believe it, Captain: in the back yard Bleek has tunneled under the building, sir, and is carrying a box marked Blasting Powder into the tunnel, sir; then downstairs in the store, sir, an Indian in a black sackcloth business suit is tending bar and calling out, 'Drink up, gents, drink up—the bar closes in fifteen seconds,' and there's a horse race at the starting-line in midstore, sir, with Trooper Fink up on that huge simple-minded Indian and Trooper Cuttlefish having the mount on Cock-eyed Hammerstein, that's Private Hammerstein, sir, Albert Sydney, serial 03J6059, sir; Hammerstein, he's six-six, sir, and Cuttlefish wouldn't go over 90 pounds in his winter woolens, sir, and, well, I would say to get your money down on our boys, sir; Fink's a good rider but that Indian has been to the bar a few times too many, sir; now, then, sir, over in one corner, past the racetrack, there's a skinny Indian in a sodbuster straw hat and overalls running a crap game, sir—and he is killing our lads, greenbacks, sir, wadded between the fingers of both hands, sir —and then this fat Indian in the poke-bonnet, sir, he is standing guard with a stone ax at the root cellar keeping our men back from the whiskey, sir; doing a bully job, I'd say; seems to have about six of our best lads laid out cold in front of the root-cellar doors and, ah, well, if you ask me, sir, I would estimate this spot to be where the main source of your ugliness is, sir; wouldn't you agree on a preliminary basis, sir, that depriving an American enlisted man of his inalienable right to buy whiskey from the Indians is a violation of his Constitutional guarantees, sir?"

During the delivery, Strinker's narrow face had turned from an apoplexy-pink to a fish-gut green.

With a vesuvian sputter, he commenced to reply to Funder's peroration. But he was superseded by a greater eruption from below. The entire building shook to the dull thump of the explosion.

"God help us!" cried Henry Milch. "The Old Crow has gone up!"

"To the catwalks! to the catwalks!" shouted Captain Strinker, trying without success to draw his saber.

"Charge!" yelled Lieutenant Funder, leaping into the breech, and forthwith leading the way out into the hall and, right-flanking it in best cavalry tradition, onward to the landing overlooking the store below.

But here courage failed. Customary pause was taken to regroup. And, within the inspiration of that halt at the stair top, Lieutenant Cumpston Funder saw beneath him the rolling, roiling tide of destiny.

Already, once that day, a smokescreen had permitted him to execute command duty with outstanding distinction, this in the matter of the surrounding and taking alive of Preacher Nehemiah Bleek. Now he saw again the black pall of opportunity. Whatever the source of the explosion, its result had been to blow the inner doors of the root cellar, and the fat Indian at stance astride their closed fortress, up into the rafters of Milch's store; that, and then the matter of the thick and choking cloud of blasting powder smoke belching up out of the breeched cellar defenses to distract the drunken troopers and to create, for the historic retreat now sprung full-grown into the fertile brain of Cumpston Funder, the perfect camouflage, the ideal military combat cover.

"Captain Strinker, sir," he whispered, fine eyes flashing. "If you and Mr. Milch will follow me, I believe we can reach the front door of the store and make our escape behind that smoke barrage loosed from the root cellar."

Strinker and Milch stared, then started up as one.

"By the Lord!" said Julius Strinker. "Lead on; you have the command, Cumpston! Genius, boy—sheer, pure, unadulterated, tactical scintillescence!"

"Thank you, Captain," blushed Funder. "It is not to every soldier that such a commanding officer comes; I am humble before your unselfish example: I do not hesitate to tell you, sir, that in my entire military—"

"Oh, for God's sake," said sutler Milch, "come on!"

And, with the rude direction, wheeled and led the way down the smoking staircase onto the field of honor below, the cavalry clanking belatedly to follow.

## 31

THE MUFFLED thump which shook the post store and sent the Cheyenne warrior, Fat, soaring, with the root-cellar doors, into the rafters of the emporium, was of course Preacher Bleek and his blasting powder.

What the Horse Creek man of frontier cloth was doing came naturally to a frugal and rational soul. He was sapping the defenses of Henry Milch's private stock to the end that what remained of its precious spirits might be expeditiously removed and loaded into the Argonaut for transport to safer, more Christian storage.

Now Preacher was blasting his way in the underground because his simple native wit told him that any open attempt to enter the building above earth, right in front of the happy patrons of the Cheyenne Bar, and cart away the bottled treasure, could only bring every hard-drinking cavalryman in the command down upon him in defense of the source of supply. And Preacher wanted that whiskey, not a renewal of his personal war with the pony soldiers in Milch's emporium.

Powder-grimed and muchly pleased, the big missionary crawled into the root cellar and seized the first case of Old Crow.

Knowing he had short time to work beneath the protective pall of the explosion, he paused only long enough to uncork one bottle and drain it in a sustained, reverent draught, before retreating upon all fours with the priceless booty.

Outside, Santiago was backing the wagon up to the excavation's mouth. *"Hijo!* you cursed *mulas!"* he cried, small brown fists full with the multiple lines of the four-animal hitch. "Don't swing out like that. Back straight, Kiowa Ladies. *Ho-shuh, ho-shuh!"* he said in near-forgotten Apache. "Gently, gently."

As brutes will with children in command, the murderous Indian mares and the man-eating Samson and Delilah put haunch to crupper and backstrap and brought the big prairie schooner to a skillful rearward dock over Preacher's sapping tunnel just as the latter emerged with the first whiskey.

On the extended tailgate of the Argonaut crouched Buzzard and Blackbird, reaching instantly for the case of Old Crow which Preacher handed upward from the hole. They stowed it with efficient teamwork into the body of the wagon and returned to the tailgate just as Preacher again popped up from the hole, a second case of the illicit spirits in tender care. So it went with the valiant salvage gamble to make certain the entire stock of undamaged bottled goods was removed from Milch's root cellar into Preacher's traveling mission. The only interruption came from Little Chief bawling on the sidelines that he had to make water. Preacher in an unguarded moment of stress, under pressure of the haste he needed to make, irately suggested to the small brother of Sunflower that he go right ahead with his project, never observing that the lad was standing on the very edge of the tunnel hole.

Naturally, Preacher did not appreciate the instant well-aimed obedience of Little Chief.

162

But such things were accepted in the hard life of a saver of Indian souls.

Or had to be under present circumstances, Preacher vowed through showered beard.

"Press on, press on!" he called cheerfully to his children, as he clambered from the tunnel hole. "Forward in the Name of the Father, the Son, and the Holy Ghost. Hallelujah!"

He stode toward the wagon's front to take the lines from Santiago. Chaining up the tailgate, Buzzard scratched his head, staring off after Preacher.

"You know," he said to Blackbird, "I know that the Father is our Lord God Jehovah, and the Son is our Dear Sweet Jesus, but I never could figure out just what in the world that Holy Ghost was."

"Oh," said Blackbird, "he's my favorite. Next to the Devil, anyway."

"Yes, you say a true thing," nodded Buzzard soberly. "That Devil is hard to beat. He's a fighter, and very crafty. Also, of course, he's an Indian."

"What? He is?"

"Of course he is. He's as red as can be."

"Oh." Frowning pause while Blackbird pondered the pigments involved. "Say, what color is that Holy Ghost?" he asked, brightening.

"White," replied the purebred Indian boy.

"Oh," nodded Blackbird. "I had hoped he might be black like me. Too bad."

"Nonsense," encouraged Buzzard. "It's a good thing. Who ever heard of a black ghost?"

"Yes, that's so," agreed the halfbreed lad, whose sire had been a Negro trooper. "Or, for that matter, a Holy buffalo soldier?"

"True, true," said bald-headed Buzzard. "Besides, I also

have a final question about all these gods in the white man's Good Book: what the hell difference does it make?"

"Does what make?"

"Which god or ghost you choose?"

"Oh, say, that's a fine question you have there, friend Buzzard. Which one do you take?"

"Maheo, every time."

"But he's an Indian god."

"And so am I an Indian."

"Ah, but I am one-half buffalo soldier. Who do the buffalo soldiers choose for a god?"

"The same as the white man."

"Why?"

"Don't ask me; ask the white man."

"Well, I did one time. I asked Preacher. He's white."

"And what did Preacher say?"

"Preacher said they did it because there were more white men than buffalo soldiers."

"Well, so are there more white men than there are Indians. But we still choose Maheo."

"That's because you—because we Indians—we have our own land and go upon it as we please."

At this answer, Buzzard once more scratched his hairless skull. "We are the owners of this land," he said, "and yet the pony soldiers don't believe it. How is that?"

"We weren't talking about pony soldiers; we were talking about buffalo soldiers. There's a big difference."

"There is? What is that?"

"The buffalo soldiers don't have any chiefs."

"Say, that's a true thing. I never thought of it before."

"Neither did I," said Blackbird. "Well, hold on tight!" He grasped a topstay as the Argonaut stirred. "There goes Preacher popping his mulewhip. Goodbye to this place."

164

"Goodbye! Goodbye!" the two boys called together, waving out the tailgate of the old freighter.

And the wagon, stirring, ceased to stir, and leaped to life full forward.

"Ho! for the mess hall!" shouted Preacher. "Ho! for the little wild children waiting there! Hi-yahh! Hi-yahh—"

And away went the Argonaut careening over the parade ground toward the beacon lamp of moonlight burnishing the panes of Kate Mehaffey's kitchen window.

# 32

RED DUST told the wild children to hurry. A bad thing had happened outside. The Round Squaw had shot an Indian who turned out to be Sergeant Schmerd, the big pony soldier with the ugly face. Round Squaw had handled the *mahaatano,* the gun-that-fires-iron-rabbit-berries, very well indeed. Now the sergeant's backside was as bad to look at as his face.

But the trouble was that Round Squaw had killed this pony soldier sergeant. And there was an unfriendly witness to the hostile act. Corporal Blemmish, the little pony soldier with the stupid face, he had seen it all. He would testify against Round Squaw and Round Squaw would be hung by a rope around her neck. That was the way the white man did such things. An Indian justice, based on reason instead of rules and regulations, would no doubt have made Round Squaw a Medicine Woman of the tribe for performing such a service, voting her a free tipi-spot and a place in the council circle for life.

White man law, however, worked differently.

If anyone killed a white man, the other white man would kill that one; and it made no difference whether the crime were foul and deserving of such punishment, or

166

were of public benefit and deserving of the common gratitude: the rope was the reward in either event.

Here, one of the wild children, a bright lad named Wild Goose Honking, interrupted to doubt that the Round White Squaw, whom the wild children called "Cannonball," was in much actual peril. Where, he wanted to know of Red Dust, would they find a rope to hold her weight? Or, again, should they learn of such a rope, what tree might they find which would not split like a green slingshot crotch when subjected to the hoisting of that great mountain of cow buffalo fat?

Red Dust did not care for such delaying conversation.

In her sleeping room, the Round Squaw was stuffing into her straw war bag such of her female fineries as might not be in ready supply aboard the Argonaut. She had entrusted to the northern boy the awakening—not awakening, really, the shotgun blasts had done that—of getting ready the wild youngsters for the dash across the parade ground.

Now let one and all roll up his or her fine cavalry blanket, putting inside of it everything of desire which might meet the Indian eye in Round Squaw's house, and so prepare to leave the pony soldier fort richer by far than they had arrived at it. No more insults of Round Squaw, who had really been very good to them all. No more cursed Indian malingering to discuss the virtues of all sides, while their own side was the only one in great danger.

Well, the idea of looting the Fort Larking mess hall and kitchens was a stroke of red genius. The Washita orphans were badly disoriented, not knowing to trust Preacher Bleek as fully as his own children, not realizing as did those children the full danger of their predicament, and the like. But they were still Cheyennes.

"I think," said Good Feather, a tiny cheerful girl of

seven or eight, "that this northern boy has stuck his thumb to the right nose this time. I am going with him. See, I take my blanket. Follow me."

The little girl spoke with unordinary authority, the others listening with accordant attention. Good Feather came from the most famed matrilineal descent among the fierce Cut Arm People. She was the ninth generation girl child to bear her name since the ancient Shahi-yena founded the tribe, successively known as the Kite, Cut Arm, and Cheyenne Indians of the Northwest Plains, in times long before the advent of the white man in that lonely and beautiful Land of the Buffalo.

"Well?" she said, stamping her small moccasin.

"Well," said Mocenimoe, Little Braid, picking up his blanket, "I agree; I take up my blanket to follow you."

"And I," announced Móeha, Grass Girl.

"Also this Indian," said Ookat, Bareskin.

"And I, and I, and I," echoed the others, and all seized up their U.S. Cavalry blankets and rushed out of the annex into the kitchen, piped like small red ratlings to the magic lure of Red Dust's Hamlin-tune of free loot for all.

Before long their blankets were bulging and Kate's kitchen assuming the bare-cupboard look of some ghost place stripped by moonlight locusts. Yet this business was taking time and the Widow Mehaffey, too, lingered overlong in the selecting of her sudden trousseau.

Nervously, Red Dust went to the window and peered out.

Well, that corporal with the vacant face was still out there. He hadn't gone for help, praise Maheo. In fact, he was working hard out there in the mess hall yard; he had gotten a shovel from somewhere and was digging a nice long square hole in the ground with a work-trooper's steady will, and more: finishing the hole, he was now

168

putting two sticks together in a crossed shape, and hammering them into the earth at one end of the hole. Remarkable.

"Hurry up," said the northern boy, turning back to the kitchen. "Tie up your blankets, now. That's enough things to take. I'm going to get Round Squaw; be ready when I return. *Nonotov, nonotov!*"

"All right," answered Wild Goose Honking. "You get The Cannonball and we will tie up our blankets. *Hai!*"

But even before Red Dust could move for Kate's bedroom, it was too late. Clear and startling in the outer night, so near also to hand that its brass notes trembled the panes in the mess hall windows, the clarion skirl of a cavalry bugle struck chill to red heart.

Good Feather spoke for the wild children of Washita River in hushed Cheyenne, the fearful memories surging back, tenfold, to hear the dreaded trumpet call once more shrilling in the dark.

"Maheo save us!" she whispered. "The pony soldiers have returned!"

Red Dust, a more cynical Cheyenne and far better educated than his simple southern cousins, glared angrily toward the Big Tipi in the Sky and shook his small fist up at the white man's God.

"Damn to hell!" he shouted. "Heap big Sweet Jesus Him do it to us again—!"

# 33

CORPORAL BLEMMISH stood lancehaft straight, bugle to quivering lip. He was not the U.S. Cavalry's premier trumpeter, a fact which might explain why Red Dust and the Washita children had thought his opening notes were those of the charge.

But they were not.

Blemmish was blowing taps over the final resting place of his departed friend, Sergeant Stanley Schmerd.

Wee Katie Mehaffey, racing from bedroom with bulging straw suitcase in time to see the panic of the Cheyenne youngsters, knew both Blemmish and the catalogue of U.S. Cavalry bugle calls better than the Indian children.

"Faith now!" she declared, "it's after being the ideal chanct to snake out the back way that the little scut is a-giving us. Don't yez all stand thir with yur eyes white-balled like a blithering bunch of remount harses! Rid Dust, tell them to layve off with thir shaking and quaking and folly along after old Kate. Shure and we'll give the carparul as foin a slip as we done to troopers Fleeb and Canister. Look aloive, yez hangdog puppies!"

170

Her rough treatment of the wild children had the steadying effect such no-nonsense handling universally achieves. Given the soft heart, the hard hand is never shied from by the young.

"Well," said Wild Goose Honking, to his cousin Good Feather, "I think we ought to go with The Cannonball."

"Yes," nodded the dark-eyed little girl. "I believe The Cannonball. She makes much noise but her tongue does not wobble." She turned to Red Dust. "Tell your Round Squaw that we will follow her; we are ready."

The northern boy repeated the agreement to Kate, who grimaced, and snorted, fat elbows akimbo, "Lah! and if the whelps had sid no, yez can tell them for me they'd have gone all the same, only wid thir haythen tales tucked betwixt thir ligs. Shooo! Scaattt! The lot of yez!"

She shooed them out the kitchen's rear exit and past the abandoned sentry post of the privy and in this way around the corner of the mess hall building, quartering across the parade ground in a line-of-march which flanked the bereaved Blemmish, thus escaping his possible challenge.

As for the latter, he was in any event too absorbed in the last rites of the gallant cavalryman who lay now at the bottom of the shallow grave in hallowed shrinement. Finishing the shivery and somewhat soured notes of taps, he laid aside the bugler's tool, retrieved that of the gravedigger. With his shovel he scooped up the first heap of earth for returning to the excavation. Pausing for one agonizing instant of tearshine, he put his hand to his heart and looked for the final time at the inscription he had composed and inscribed upon the rude cross which stood above all human that remained of Stanley Schmerd.

HERE LAYS S.K. SCHMERD
SGT. OF U.S. CAV. WHUT
WAS DID IN FROM BEHIND
GOODBYE STANLEY

Then, the farewell tribute paid, Blemmish tossed the
first shovelful graveward. The clods showered down without mercy, falling upon the waxen face of him who rested
there on tortured hams in slumber deep but hardly permanent. With the fine small grit and pebbles still trickling
from the side of the hole, Stanley Schmerd reared up from
the grave spitting Kansas clay and limestone chunks in
fair good time to take a second shovelful of digger's earth
square in his pale but raging face.

"You idiot!" he roared at Blemmish. "Get me out of
here!"

172

# 34

Leading the way down the staircase from his second-floor quarters, storekeeper Henry Milch saw that the smoke from the mined root cellar lay perfectly to cover the escape. Motioning to Strinker and Funder to keep low, he zigzagged across the open field, skirted the pot-bellied stove, dived safely behind the counter of Harness & Home Remedies. The two bare-shanked officers followed him in, and the first ground was won.

"Now," whispered Milch, "we must get through Gent's Furnishings to Ladies Wear, then via Ammunition & Dried Fruits to the front door. As you can see, there's a bit of open ground between each. But with those boobs all over there fighting the smoke to see what happened, we have a chance to make our escape."

"Yes, yes, for God's sake!" squeaked Strinker. "We can see the route. Lead on."

"If you think you can do better, Julius," Milch began haughtily. But the C.O. cut him short, and the advance resumed. Gent's Furnishings was reached without incident. The front door and freedom lay but forty feet away.

"All right," ordered General Milch, warming to the strange great feel of command. "Follow me, close order, single file, no loud talk and—"

"Oh, for Heaven's sake!" gritted Funder. "Go ahead."

Milch led off. Mid-way of the open ground, he stole a glance over his shoulder toward the far end of the store and the continuing commotion around the Cheyenne Bar and bombed-out root cellar. The hairs at the nape of his neck came erect with individual and quivering life.

"Don't panic," he told his companions. "But the wind has changed and the smoke is shifting. This is it, men. Keep a steady pace. Act as though nothing had happened."

He went back onto his belly and wormed the remaining ten feet into Ladies Wear with a looping speed which would have shamed a hoop snake on the high roll in front of a prairie fire.

"That's a steady pace?" said Strinker to Funder.

"No sir," answered the young lieutenant. "This is."

And with the explanation, Cumpston Funder brought down his elevated buttocks and dry-swam the remaining way, flat to floorboards, in an elapsed time to make the sutler's dash seem leisurely.

Left alone, Julius Strinker first knew a moment's classic fear, then made his own decision. It was in the tradition of the Strinker military men, the heritage of the command presence. *"Wait for me!"* he bawled in a strangulated whisper. And, forthwith, flopped over on his spine and propelled himself on his back with short shoves of both feet into the haven of Ladies Wear.

Rejoined, the Soldiers Three knew a moment's reprise.

At the far end of the store the reeling troopers waited above ground while scouts were sent below into the root cellar to learn of the damage control report from the now smoke-clearing shelves of Bottled Goods.

"Now, men," Milch began again, but again Funder cut him rudely short.

174

"Oh, be still, Henry. Whose idea was this, anyway?"

"Yes," supported Strinker, also recovering his aplomb with the front door so near. "Without Cumpston's brilliant inspiration, we should still all be crouching up in your odious quarters waiting for those riotous brutes to corner us and contaminate, perhaps terminally, our command images. What was it you were about to say, Cumpston?"

From his position, prone behind the screening counter of Ladies Wear, Lieutenant Funder scraped his elbow along the floor to snap a proper salute. "With your permission, Captain," he said, "I should like to resume command here."

"Permission granted," saluted Strinker proudly.

"*Now*, men," said Funder, smirking in triumph at Milch, "follow *me*." He started to inch out from the counter but was halted by the appearance of a band of Indians retreating by the same route, or rather toward the same exit. The warriors did not see the pony soldier lieutenant draw back behind Ladies Wear, and so passed swiftly on to Ammunition & Dried Fruits. There, however, they did take halt, thus delaying yet more fatefully the departure of the Fort Larking staff officers and their faithful post sutler from the cover of Ladies Wear.

"Listen," the crouching white men heard the leader of the Indian force, say to his followers, "we no can leave Cheyenne brother in lurch."

"We no leave him in lurch," argued a fellow. "We leave him up on rafter."

"*Hau!*" grunted one of the others. "*He-hau*, damn to hell. Let's go. Him no blame us. Blame Preacher. We no blow up whiskey cave."

"Him Cheyenne brother," repeated the leader stubbornly.

"Not this Cheyenne's brother," chimed in the fourth

warrior. "Me part Kiowa. Goodbye."

The first brave seized the defector by the throat.

"Yellow Nose say me leader!" he growled. "You do what Cross Feather him tell you."

At this juncture the other two Indians drew from beneath their various borrowed white attires two looted articles of war, a wooden-handled butcher knife and a Chicago boning cleaver. "Good," rumbled Dog Chips, flourishing the housewife's friend, while his comrade Stick-of-Wood brandished the meat cleaver. "What Cross Feather tell him to do?"

Given the option of loyalty to the high-stranded Fat, or dismemberment on the spot, Cross Feather decided against fraternal solidarity.

"Me tell him run like hell," he declared honestly.

And, suiting action to advice, he led the exodus of retiring Smoky Hill bartenders through Ammunition & Dried Fruits, on the wild-pony gallop, to the front door and into the outer night.

"Phew!" said Milch, swabbing his beaded brow. "That was close."

"Tight lip, men," said Funder, tersely. "Move out."

But the halt at Ladies Wear had been fatal.

At the far end of the store the drunken troopers had discovered the nature of Preacher Bleek's treacherous whiskey theft in the same moment that they heard the dangling Cheyenne warrior, Fat, cry out plaintively for his fleeing fellows to return and take him with them, like true Indian brothers. Peering with bloodshot eyes from Fat to his vanishing friends, they were in time to see Cross Feather and the others bolt out the front of the store.

With the awesome abdominal roar of the betrayed mob, they surged toward the exit and vengeance on the whiskey-peddling red men. Their reeking tide thundered past, then lapped back on, Ladies Wear, trapping the terrified Funder, Milch and Strinker in cowering panic behind the frail counter.

# 35

From his airy vantage high in the rafters of Milch's store, the abandoned Cheyenne warrior had an eagle's view of the fray; the smoky lamplighted diorama spread below his aerie hid no secret of troop or temper from the fat one's powder-burned gaze.

He saw the noble Cross Feather yield to blackmail of butcher knife and cleaver. Saw all four of his deserting comrades battle to be first through the door. Saw, also, Julius Strinker, Henry Milch and Cumpston Funder cowering, unseen by soldier, amid corset, camisole, skirt, slip, petticoat, and lacewear undefined by Cheyenne tongue. And saw, as well, the muttering surge of the cheated trooper mob spill out the front door in pursuit of the fleeing red bartenders. Saw the mob swirl briefly in the outer night, return through door into the store, eluded by the swift Cheyenne, begin once more to hunger and to growl aloud for redress, blurred vision seeking other prey, and easier, than the vanished sons of the Smoky Hill. And then Uxtato, known as Fat, saw the last and strangest thing of all. Behind the counter and beneath the racks where fancy things of the white squaw were for sale, the fertile brain of Cumpston Funder had been teeming once again. The seed of last salvation was asprout. Young Funder transplanted its germ by a frantic whisper to Strinker and Milch. Both men recoiled at first, as though the young lieutenant had spat, not murmured hotly, against their lobes. Then both as eagerly recovered. While Fat still smoldered on his rafter, staring down, the puny one-bar chief of pony soldiers, his naked-bottomed captain and the whiskey–smuggling sutler of the only mail-order store in western Kansas, began painting-up and putting on the flowered hats, high-button shoes, and bustle-padded dresses of the paleface female.

## 36

"TAKE THE pink taffeta," advised storekeeper Milch, studying Cumpston Funder's complexion. "With your interestingly pale face it should be stunning."

"Well," demanded Captain Strinker, impatiently, "how about me? I'm here, too, you know!"

"You," said Milch, "keep your voice down. There are *others* still here, too, you know!"

There were indeed.

In front of the counter and at both ends angry soldiers swarmed. They were now commencing to ransack the store—not looting it, but rather conducting a desperate search for an overlooked supply of medicinal spirits. Some of them were beginning to break things, to hurl merchandise about, emptying shelves for no reason but to vent their spleen first at Bleek's blue-nosed blasting heavenward of the root cellar—the Argonaut had been seen pulling away from the hole into the cellar—and then by the successful sneak-out of the Cheyenne bartenders and gambling shills and racetrack touts, under cover of Preacher's whip-popping dash away from the sabotage job. Given such frustration, it would seem Milch's statement would be self-evident; but Strinker, at least, and to a lesser degree his brainy aide, Funder, were men of more than

180

simple military tastes, and their talents ran elsewhere than to strictly combat problems or conditions.

"Yes, yes," Strinker now whispered in response to the merchant's warning against loud talk in ranks. "I see what you mean. But my dear Milch, I simply must have something decent to wear. I will not go out in just any old rag."

"Shut up," groaned Milch. "Let me think."

As he pondered, young Funder convoluted on his skinny belly from beneath the counter to beneath the dress rack of Ladies Wear. Strinker and Milch could see him wriggling upward from the floor, seeming to arise like an East India cobra from the basket of the snakecharmer, to disappear into the confines of the pink taffeta. "Capital!" cried Strinker. "Superb on you, Cumpie!"

"Idiot!" hissed Milch, and clapped a desperate hand to the captain's enthusiastic mouth.

Fortunately for all three, a moment's diversion was granted with the discovery behind the Cheyenne Bar of some bottles of unbroken Old Crow. Here was one last sip at Bacchus' best bourbon, all around, and while the thirsting garrison took pause to share it out, Henry Milch made mail-order fashion history.

"Julius," he said to Strinker, "for you I suggest the flowered chintz with feather boa. With it, I think the eight-button saffron kid shoe. And I think the black opera gloves with a lilac kerchief at the wrist. The hat will be that *Eugenie* with the blue dotted-swiss veil."

Strinker, following the master's selections, curled a suspicious lip. "Isn't that a bit stuffy for *me?*" he objected. "After all, I'm no matron, you know."

"You're a milk-legged widow, about thirty," calmed Milch. "With a wandering shy glance and a double-pad Philadelphia bustle. All right?"

181

"Oh, wonderful!" cried the captain, and writhed across the aisle to disappear beneath the dress rack.

Not waiting for him to complete his grass widow's weeds, Milch scuttled crabwise over the floor to the rack and made his own choices—a daring décolleté ballgown from Spiegelglass of Chicago, with matching patent leather dance pumps fastening ankle-high with *straps!*

For a nasty moment, when Strinker saw the anklestrap pumps, things turned green. But Milch, quick of brain as any shopkeeper, and with the merchant's instant instinct to keep the customer happy while picking his purse, at once promised him that if he did not like his yellow-kid high buttons he might exchange them next day for the black ballroom pumps, at no extra charge.

Pleased, the C.O. subsided.

Cumpston Funder, striking in the wild-rose pink, with a sheared swamprat shako by Daché of Paris—Sam Daché of Paris, Kentucky—again took command of the expedition at Strinker's blushing request. Cumpie *was* lovely in pink. Funder, for his part, was still all soldier, all intent upon a successful conclusion to the bold gambit to cross the parade ground disguised as—well, not really 'ladies of the evening,' as might first seem, but more in the nature of, say, Godey Girls astroll by starlight. First, however, by whatever name or in whatever guise, the front door of Henry Milch's emporium must be safely reached, and negotiated.

Now, Cumpston saw, darting an eagle-eye toward the Cheyenne Bar, was the moment sent by Mars.

Up! Soldiers Three, away!

Out from under the dress rack, into the back-counter aisle, crawled the mail-order gals. Down the narrow musty aisle they hunched their swift way to the counter's

182

end and the dash thus to Ammunition & Dried Fruits and the front door, there to effect the final standing up and graceful swaying exit on their feet and unafraid—indeed, untouchable. They were ladies. And this was the West.

But the true test was never run.

Midway of Ladies Wear stood an alcove in the dress rack formed by floor-length mirrors set at three angles to show milady what she looked like fore, aft and broadside, in her new *maladresse* from the Maison Milch.

No deadlier trap might have been laid for the last masker in the crawling military line. When Funder and Milch made safe scuttle to Ammunition & Dried Fruits, took a deep breath, stood up, promenaded out the door and made it safely into the dark of night, they whirled about, as one, to congratulate the following post commander, only to find that he was not following.

By common premonition, both men pressed their faces to the storefront window, horrified glances glued to Ladies Wear and the three French full-length mirrors.

There he was, caught like Alice, in the looking glass.

Unable to resist the temptation in bellying by it on the floor, Julius Caesar Strinker had stood up, all unconscious of the mortal danger of the moment, to preen and spy at himself in his flowered chintz and feathered boa. And, even as his two accomplices stood paralyzed at the pane, the reeling louts of Fort Larking's refreshed garrison discovered they had, indeed, overlooked something in their search of the store for spirit stimulants.

One hairy-brisketed celebrant, stumbling away from the now truly droughted-out Cheyenne Bar, stared toward Ladies Wear. He shook his head, stared again, blinked open both red eyes and bugged them à la bullfrog.

"*Good Gawd Amighty!*" he breathed in almost-prayer.

183

Then, recovering, he roared in the bellow of a rutting buffalo. "*YeeeEEE-haaHH!* Stand back, boys; I seen her first—!"

Outside the store, Funder and Milch read what was in the soldier's randy mind. They saw, as well, what was on the faces of the other troopers stampeding after the first man. The temper of the mob, stationed on the endless plains of western Kansas for seventeen months, was not to be confused with ordinary male urges. It was suddenly, libidinously clear to the willowy lieutenant and his dumpy companion that whatever wore a skirt that night within the stockade of Fort Larking did so at the peril of considerably more than loss of enlisted respect.

"I believe," said Cumpston Funder, "that I shall be of more service to my captain by fighting my way to the duty post across the parade ground, there to change into proper uniform and seize back command of this post."

"Call it what you want," nodded Henry Milch, hoisting his ballgown and tensing the toe of his shiny pump. "Just don't get in my way, boy!" And with the admonition, the sutler sprinted off into the night bound for points and parts unknown, but free of lusting trooper.

"Coward!" shrilled Funder.

And, hiking up his pink taffeta, set sail with feather boa streaming for places far from Captain Julius Caesar Strinker and his date with destiny behind the counter of Ladies Wear.

# 37

CAPTAIN STRINKER gave a female scream and fled. The flowered chintz was little handicap, as it split the lower seam, hem to waistband, on the officer's first agonized leap toward freedom. The pursuing soldiers no doubt took wonder at the bent and hairy nature of this damsel's legs exposed fetchingly by the Shanghai side-slit of the chintz gown. But still the muscles and bristles and Indian-like bow of Strinker's limbs were capped by the flashing eight-button yellow shoes. And who, seventeen months beyond legal view of white woman, could misread the meaning of that lavendar kerchief at the wrist of the fleeing sylph?

Scream or no scream, this gorgeous milk-white filly was fair game. She was going to get haltered and forelocked and flung down, by damn, or the U.S. Cavalry would know the reason why not.

Knowing the reason why not, of course, was what coursed in panic through the mind of Julius Caesar Strinker.

If the men ever learned of his masquerade, he would not only lose his rank and command—he could easily lose his life, as wild-eyed drunk as these hooting bullies were.

Yet, again, it was the very abandon of their binge which prevented the pursuing troopers from bringing him immediately to bay. Many as they were, they stumbled and fumbled and bumbled with such hearty success that the quick-toed captain was able to elude seven separate charges in as many zigzagging dashes from one counter to the other. Indeed, the men were so totally fusel-oiled that when, on the eighth rush, one of their number actually seized Strinker, the brute gave his C.O. a resounding buss and, being simultaneously kneed by the captain, threw up his arms and cried out in stupored agony that he had felt that embrace all the way down to the blinking fundament. And, naturally, when he released the slippery hussy to fling his arms high with ecstasy, the trollop ducked and fled into the ninth trap, a leering circle of slack-jawed brutes who closed about the frantic lass to pen her beneath the staircase to the upper floor.

This was an historic moment.

For in its same instant of ambush Fat, the forgotten Cheyenne, frightened by the mad chase below, had decided to desert his rafter. As Strinker cowered beneath the stairway, Fat trod airily along his beam to the banistered landing of the stairs at the head of the second-floor hallway. Leaping the banister like some pot-bellied ignoble stag at eve, the Indian made off down the hallway as fast as his stumpy bowed limbs would bear him. But he had been seen. Over the heads of the ravening jackal pack closing upon him, the desperate officer caught a fleeting glimpse of Fat's vault over the banister to the upper hallway landing. The maneuver returned to Strinker's mind memory of the strong door and solid locking bar of Henry Milch's boudoir. By the gods of war! if he could but reach the upper hall and gain down it into Milch's room ahead of the rutting troopers, all might yet be won. Once in the room, the door bar holding the soldiers long enough, he could disrobe himself of female clutter and emerge, even sans pants, as a reasonable facsimile of the captain commanding.

It was all the chance he had in any sense.

And even to seize that slim option, he must first break free of the jack-booted lechers now pawing toward him in his darkest recess of the staircase angle.

No weapon was at hand. No way out by speed of foot or agile twist of winsome shape. Here the sheer power of the superior mind must obtain, or a fate far uglier than court-martial must ensue. Strinker's cunning, honed by family tradition and selective breeding for the recessive genes of cupidity and survival, did not fail him now. In a last glance, his walling eye fell upon the lavender dab of perfumed cloth at his gloved wrist. Whipping high the dainty wisp, he balled it hard in his sweaty palm, flung it out over the yammering heads of the salacious cavalry pack. His trilling soprano rang like a silver bell with a heart of tin, a laugh as false as his falsetto, yet in that time and place a veritable siren song to bloody combat.

"May the best man wear it on his lance, dear lads!" he cried. "And remember—*winner takes all!* Tee-hee."

There was a moment's deathly-still pause, during which the lavender hanky fluttered into the maw of the molesting soldier mob. Then, even as the wolf pack turns upon itself when one is wounded or a leader falls, the troopers dove after the token in one snarling instant free-for-all converging on their common center. Wincing to the frightful uproar, Strinker tiptoed out from under the stair, around the cornerpost of the stairflight to the second floor, and was gone up the risers silent as a lady shade, already knowing that he had won the awesome risk.

When, midway of flight, a drunken outcry from below let him know the troops had seen his path and would at once bound upward on it, Strinker only smiled and scarce increased his lope. When, however, that lope brought him to the hallway's dimming end, letting him see that the Cheyenne known as Fat was crouching there before him, and when Fat, alarmed by this unexpected appearance so close upon the heels of his own escape, seized the knob of the wrong hallway door—not that of Milch's room—the white captain's shrill cry turned a thing of naked terror.

"No, no, my God, not *that* one—!" he shrieked, and was forever too late.

Fat swung wide the door to the building's outer landing, with its flight of stairs to the earth below.

Upon the landing, faithful to the station assigned him by his master, Nehemiah Bleek, the savage Lame Wolf crouched to spring past the startled Fat, who, after all, smelled like an Indian, to charge down the hallway after his primer-scented prey: white meat!

Strinker gargled his fear, unable even to find voice for it. Wheeling, he drove back toward the landing. Reaching it, just as he was about to be borne under by the first wave of laboring soldiers and the fetid fangs of a Cheyenne killer-dog, he was able to spring free of the landing, out upon Fat's vacated rafter. Along this slender spiderweb strand he raced for life, or very least for limb.

Behind him, the frustrated Cheyenne man-eater turned his yellow-orbed fury on the upward-staggering herd of drunken cavalrymen. Ah, more white meat! and marinated.

If he could not have a captain, he would take these fifty-or-so enlisted men—it mattered little to Lame Wolf. The Indian recognized no rank, exercised no discrimination, gave equal treatment to all. And he trained his dog in his own image. A democratic dog. A people's dog. A dog entirely without bigotry or bias or taint of any class

188

or racial prejudice.

Such a dog was noble Lame Wolf, hero-canine of the hostile Cut Arm Nation.

Entirely without malice, he forthwith charged the staircase-channeled garrison of the last fort west in Kansas.

The U.S. Cavalry panicked, broke, fell back in utter disorder. Lame Wolf galloped the length of the store through their scattering ranks, never breaking stride, and ran on out into the night baying as best he could with great jaws loaded with pony soldier pants, muffled Cheyenne basso profundo proclaiming to the Indian world that the whites had taken another red shellacking.

Captain J.C. Strinker, under Indian-given cover of this diversion, abandoned the narrow field of Fat's rafter and made Milch's bedroom unseen.

When, after regrouping, the sobered but still salty servicemen remembered the trim flossie of their interrupted chase, they again invaded the second floor in search of her. There they broke down merchant Milch's bar-locked boudoir door only to find an indignant Captain Strinker, sans pants and bare-to-buff beneath, but still otherwise clad in Custer fringe shirt, full-booted, with black wideswept hat, shielding as only an officer and a gentleman might their lowly view from the hallway of the bed of Henry Milch. Well, 'fore God, what was a red-blooded U.S. hairy-eared horse soldier to do save to snap to and salute a better man, by thunder, and quicker than themselves?

That sure as shooting wasn't Henry Milch lumping up the covers of that yonder bed so shapely, and all.

Those certain as sin weren't the sutler's duds hanging over the bed's foot, all flowered chintz, eight-button yellow shoes and double Philadelphia bustle pads.

And that absolutely as sunrise or sunset or water running where the slope lay was not the passionate-pink perfume of anything named Milch, which smote their furry nostrils from behind their captain's back.

To a man, the Fort Larking garrison stood-to in parade-brace and gave five stiff salutes to the man who, quietly, competently, boldly and at a single stroke, had won it all.

"*Captain, sir,*" said one of them, the humbled voice saying it for all, and with a pride to lump the larynx of any cavalry commander alive, "*your men salute you—!*"

There were no more words, then, as Strinker took the touching tribute, and returned it.

Someone in the ranks commenced softly to whistle the brave strains of "Gary Owen," Custer's regimental marching song, and the men, file-by-file, turned away and double-timed along the hallway and down the staircase, never looking back, or needing to.

They would always remember their captain standing there in his buckskins, bare bottom and black hat.

# 38

THE ARGONAUT had only commenced to roll in its dash across the parade ground toward the mess hall and the rescue of the Washita wild children, when Sunflower burst into sudden loud clamor: faithful Lame Wolf had been forgotten; they had abandoned him still on his post of war, the upper landing of the outside stairway to Milch's second-floor quarters.

Preacher knew better than to argue with the Arapaho girl. She had a secret weapon, her small brother Little Chief, which she might turn upon Bleek. Moreover, she was the Horse Creek giant's special pet, and he would drive through the portals of Satan's Hades for her, let alone merely to haul about on the dead gallop a four-animal freight-hitch and go back to get the missing wolf dog.

Ho, Samson! Ho, Delilah! Ho, you Kiowa Ladies!

Bleek stood up on the driver's box yelling for all to hang on, and swung his teams in a turn which threw up a sickle-shaped dust cloud visible for miles in the clear prairie moonlight. Thundering back toward the store, he brought up the wheezing Argonaut at the foot of the outer stair just in time to see the five Smoky Hill peace delegates he had commissioned, via Big Baby, to open the Cheyenne

Bar, come galloping out of the store in their various white man's attire and vanish in the moonhaze. Before he might recover from this sight, Funder and Milch dashed out and away in their frontier ladies' finery. And, no sooner were they fading through the murk toward the main gate command post, than Lame Wolf came howling out of the store to tongue his victory into lunar space.

Little Sunflower, riding with Preacher on the driver's seat, put her chubby fingers into her small mouth to blast the piercing whistle with which she called the brute to heel. But Preacher, watching the shaggy one, halted her. "Hold," he said. "Mark how the dog is starting to quarter. He's on the track of something, honey. Leave him run. See! Yonder he goes, lining out after them two floozies."

Sunflower could see, all right, but still wanted her dog. Preacher convinced her that no harm could come to Lame Wolf which Lame Wolf would not return tenfold to the bringer. Meanwhile, their greater duty lay to free her little wild cousins from the mess hall. To go and get the Washita children and race with them, all safe in the Argonaut, back out of Fort Larking's main gate and away to the Smoky Hill River camp of Spotted Wolf and the free Cheyenne.

Did not Sunflower remember that Preacher had promised the wild children this delivery?

Was it not Preacher's fault that they were all presently trapped in the stockade of the pony soldier camp?

Would it honor any of them who were of the old Horse Creek School—any of the original children of Nehemiah Bleek and the Colorado beginnings—to fail the Washita orphans? How might the Horse Creek children better prove their teachings in outwitting the white man, than to get those poor lost babes of Black Kettle's murdered band away from Fort Larking? Away from the fort and safely brought, at last, to the longing arms of their wild kinfolk? Those wild kinfolk who were waiting even now in sleepless anxiety the word which their peace mission to the Kansas pony soldier post would return to them? Would it not be a wondrous thing if Yellow Nose, Cross Feather, Big Baby, Dog Chips, Stick-of-Wood, and Fat could go back to the Smoky Hill and say that Preacher Bleek and his orphans of the Arkansas had beaten the U.S. Cavalry? Had reduced Fort Larking to a rubble of whiskey bottles and mule marbles? Why, *iho!* the people would be painting pictures of it on the tipi skins for the next hundred winters!

Away with Lame Wolf. Let him run his own track.

Their track lay toward the mess hall and the rescue of the Washita wild children.

Ho, for the mess hall!

When Preacher finished, there wasn't a dry eye in the Argonaut. Sunflower, Buzzard, Blackbird, Santiago all cheered and choked-up in Indian unison; and Little Chief stood, freehand, upon the jolting tailgate of the ancient freighter and made his watermark, unbroken, from Milch's store to the sight of the company kitchen, across the total dusty span—almost—of Captain Julius Caesar Strinker's pony soldier command.

## ▲▲▲▲▲▲▲▲▲▲ 39

FUNDER'S SPIRITS soared even as he loped ahead of Henry Milch toward the main gate. If this would seem perverse, considering his position, the native genius of Cumpston Funder could be blamed. Ordinary men could not fathom it. The young lieutenant himself was most frequently startled by its manifestations.

Such as presently.

Escaping from the very jaws of disgrace, avoiding by the whim of the martial gods, alone, the fate which must surely have come to Captain Julius Strinker by now, Funder had before him horizons limited only by the splendid burst of creative thought now dazzling his brain.

All that he had to do was alter his course a point or three of the compass, bearing for the post infirmary rather than the deserted main gate command post. At the infirmary, he would request—he would command—Major Hummerbund, the post surgeon, to issue fit-for-active-duty tickets on the eight or ten men Bleek had put into the sick ward with his wild defense of the redoubt in Milch's store. Then, with these wounded heroes to back him, Funder would race for the main gate, close it and bar it and stand by with the infirmary squad to die in its defense. Trapping Bleek and his Indian children—Goverment property, remember—and stolen at that—would follow neatly. Subduing them and restoring the post to order, supported by Strinker's troops if need be, must ensue logically. All that remained beyond this could be entrusted to the cavalrymen who, meanwhile, would have uncovered the C.O.'s masquerade as the *haute couture* harlot of the Arkansas and would surely crucify their captain with their testimony at the subsequent inquiry conducted by the Inspector General.

If this sequence inspired by the original mind of Lieutenant Cumpston Funder did not result in said Funder being promoted to permanent rank and given the command at Fort Larking, then Bleek was not crazy and Strinker no popinjay.

But, lo! even as the future beckoned, the past clammered fearfully behind.

The long wolflike wailing of the great Cheyenne cur, Lame Wolf, rose into the night. Glancing fearfully toward the post store, both Milch and Funder saw the howling brute at the same time. The way that he ran through the moonlight, nose glued to the ground along the very trackline laid down by themselves within the minute, let the fugitives know that their time on that parade ground was numbered.

"Get out of my way!" yelled Milch, and sprinted past the lieutenant, clearly bound for the open main gate and the freedom of the outer prairies.

Perhaps it was the storekeeper's craven bid to save self which triggered the foul deed in Funder's mind. Perhaps the dark plan would have sprung from such teeming soil in any event, given the goose-pimpling basso of Lame Wolf's wild cry. No matter. On the instant, Funder knew he must survive. If Henry Milch had to be thrown to the half-wolf, as it were, so be it. But the fate of Fort Larking, the integrity of the U.S. Cavalry, the very image of the United States Government upon the frontier, was at stake. *Funder had to live.* To live, and to decide, in the swift instants still separating the two men from the Indian dog, by what manner best to employ the cowardly sutler's life in the service of his country.

He saw his answer looming slenderly ahead: the fort's flagpole implanted in front of the main gate command post.

Whipping his weary muscles, Funder came abreast of Henry Milch by a last, superb burst of energy. As he did, he artfully stuck his foot betwixt both those of the flying Milch. The storekeeper went bustle-over-Spiegelglass ballgown. It was a magnificent trip, cartwheeling him into the base of the flagpole, ringing his skull against the rusted iron and landing him flat on his back with his anklestrap dancing pumps straddling the pole. It was but the work of a moment for the agile Funder to snare one of the storekeeper's ankles in a loop of the flagpole's halyard and, hauling away with a manly will, to run Milch up the flagpole and leave him there, full-mast and flapping, in the night wind.

As for himself, Funder lit out on the high lope for the infirmary. He gambled that mighty Lame Wolf, finding his quarry treed, would hold up to bay the flagpole, giving Funder time to reach the men in Hummerbund's hospital. After that, he gave no least commander's damn for Lame Wolf, or any other power of the prairie night.

Coming to the Cheyenne killer-dog, the lieutenant was in luck.

Intelligence had never contributed to the animal's reputation. He was a fighter, not a figurer. When he raced up to the foot of the flagpole to espy the storekeeper adangle by one foot from the topmost halyard, he reared to brace his forepaws on the rusted pole, making the night a bedlam with the outburst of his howls.

"Beautiful!" sighed Cumpston Funder, looking back over his pink taffeta shoulder; and let out the last notch in his lope toward the Fort Larking infirmary.

# 40

Now PREACHER BLEEK, driving the Argonaut like a county fair racing sulky, was almost to the mess hall. Suddenly Santiago, riding astride black Samson, the giant lead-mule, cried out and raised his hand. Selected to perch on the big mule as advance lookout because of his Apache-keen eyesight, the little *mestizo* lad had sighted something. It was, he informed Preacher in high-pitched Spanish of the *monte*, Red Dust and the wild children of the Washita. They were coming on the run toward the Argonaut. *Miran! Miran!* They had escaped. Hurry, Preacher, hurry! The pursuit was only just behind Red Dust and those Washita cousins.

"Pursuit?" frowned Preacher, standing with the reins to the pitch and sway of the old freighter. "What pursuit?"

"There!" shouted Santiago, pointing over the heads of the approaching children. "Don't you see? In the dust not twenty strides behind. Going very rough but strong. Even with that heavy suitcase of straw she is carrying. *Hijo!*"

"She?" said Preacher, feeling his broad belly pinch-in and grow small with the possibility Santiago's mention of the loaded suitcase suggested to his bachelor's imagination. "What do you mean, 'she'? Quickly, now, *niño!* Who is it?"

"Why," yelled the halfbreed boy, "it's she, the very round squaw, the one the wild children call 'The Cannonball.'"

"God in Heaven!" cried Preacher Bleek.

Here, Sunflower, seeking to calm the Horse Creek missionary, reminded him that the Washita waifs, being wild Indians, would be able to make a running mount of the Argonaut. This the fat white squaw could not duplicate. Thus, all Preacher need do was wheel the wagon in a sweeping loop to come across the front of the running children, signaling Red Dust to lead them in a true Cheyenne boarding of the moving vehicle. In this way, surely, the children could be snatched from out the very talons of the huge-rumped, short white she-bear who was chasing them.

"Lord Gawd Amighty!" lamented Preacher, panic-stricken, "that's just the trouble! She ain't chasing them kids; she's chasing me!"

The significance of this was lost on Sunflower. But the practical merit of her proposed pick-up of the fugitive Cheyenne orphans was not lost on Bleek. With a roaring "Geeeee!" which shattered the nerves even of the wicked Samson, he swung the lead-mules in a right-turning arc toward the racing children. Another bull-rut roar to Red Dust brought an answering shout of understanding from the nephew of Roman Nose, who promptly guided his small followers in a hawing maneuver so to place them on a matching course with the lumbering freight wagon. Entering into the Indian spirit of the thing, the Washita children ran like coyote cubs. Red Dust had timed their turn precisely and, with the reaching hands of the Horse Creek orphans extended to them from the wagon, all were able to board the Argonaut without a slip or stumble.

Joining Preacher on the driver's box, the northern boy

looked back and waved affectionately to the vanishing form of Kate Mehaffey, a-struggle at a losing pace to the wagon's rear.

"It is too bad," he said in dignified Cheyenne to the grizzly-coated Bleek. "She is a better squaw than she looks. Very kind to the Washita children. They respected her, even. So did I. Without her, not one of us would have reached this wagon. And she is in bad trouble, too."

Bleek naturally had to inquire as to what this talk was all about. And when, in an Indian's clear and lucid way, Red Dust told him of the Cheyenne indebtedness to Mrs. Dennis Mehaffey, ending with the lady's killing of the miserable Sergeant Schmerd, Preacher understood that a moral decision of first magnitude was upon him.

He made it with the simple judgment that was his.

Up he reared on the driver's box again. Once more the thunderous "Geeee!" echoed over the post. And again the Argonaut circled to the right and, on this second lap, picked up the badly-winded Irish cook and washerwoman of Fort Larking, her ample bulk welcomed aboard by a dozen small dark hands reaching to help her.

"Swayte Jazus!" panted Wee Katie, tumbling in over the tailgate. "Bliss yez, me dusky darlings, ivry wan of yez."

Then, catching the wall-eyed glance of apprehension flung back her way by Bleek through the forward pucker-hole of the careening Argonaut, she smoothed her corn-shuck curlers, her horsefeed-sacking negligee, and the gunbore grease and gopher fat beauty cream which anointed her orange freckles.

"Faith, now, Praycher dear," she warbled. "And shure I was after thinking I nivver would ketch up to yez, yez darlin' man. Bejabbers, lad, yez'll nivver regrat it!"

"God help us!" groaned Preacher Bleek, and poured the blacksnake whip to Samson and the wheelers.

200

**41**

"What is that thing flapping from the flagpole?" asked Big Baby of his friend Dog Chips.

The five Indians, escaping from Milch's store, were approaching the main gate feeling their way warily along the base of the stockade. They were almost free, but curiosity had killed more Plains Indians than cats. Dog Chips broke stride, peered through the starlight.

"Why, I can't say," he replied. "From the sound of that dog of Preacher's, however, I would guess it is something the cur has treed. Isn't that that tame wolf of his, leaping there at the bottom of the pole?"

"Yes, yes," said Stick-of-Wood. "That is surely Preacher's dog. Come on, everybody. Let us go see what he has put up the flagpole."

"We'd better keep going for the gate," objected Fat, but no one listened to him. Even Cross Feather, the leader, was veering out from the stockade's shadow to cross over to the pole implanted in front of Strinker's office. "Oh, well," shrugged the rotund brave, whose white blood had warned him to not dally, "after all, I, too, am an Indian. I may as soon go along and see the fun as the next Cheyenne."

At the flagpole, they halted peering intently upward.

They paid no heed to Lame Wolf's snarling antics, nor did the huge dog give them a second glance, once his keen nose had informed him they were red men and not on his diet list.

"*Hau, nisen,* hello there, friend," called out Big Baby. "Who are you hanging upside down like a bat flapping your wings?"

"Buffalo calf!" snorted Dog Chips, shoving him aside. "He doesn't speak or understand our tongue. Here, I will talk to him in his own language." He stepped forward, an important fellow for the moment. "What hell you do him up there?" he challenged Milch. "You want come down?"

The storekeeper, weak from struggling, dizzy from hanging head-down, managed to convey to the braves that he would pay anything within reason to be released. The Indians discussed it and decided they would take down the whiskey-smuggling white man and conduct him as a prisoner to their big winter camp on the Smoky Hill River. There they would try him for the crime of possessing the *vehoemap* for obvious sale to the red brother of the Arkansas. Whiskey had nearly ruined the Cheyenne nation and although the five warriors loved their tin trade cup of Kentucky Corn as dearly as the next Indian, they also understood that white men such as Henry Milch had destroyed more of them than Custer and Chivington put together. No less an authority—both on war and whiskey-drinking—than their own great war chief, the wily Spotted Wolf, had said that the white man's fiery *vehoemap* was the most remarkable invention since squaws. It killed men more surely than any bullet, yet made them to die happy all the same.

The conversation being in Cheyenne, Milch made out no word of it, but was only vastly relieved to know the red devils were there and had mentioned bringing him down.

202

But the Smoky Hill men were tired. They were also a very long way from home, and they did not have their horses to ride. However, as they turned to leave Milch on the pole and make for the gate, who should totter in through that same opening but Yellow Nose—and leading their six ponies behind him.

The little Ute chief had fallen in a haystack just outside the fort and, save for his powder-burned pride, was little the worse for his wild skyrocket ride over the stockade wall. He now handed over to the braves their shaggy mounts, suggesting that long tracks be made for Smoky Hill.

"No, wait!" cried Big Baby, always thinking. "Now that we have our ponies, we can carry along that storekeeper. Yellow Nose has already said he himself cannot sit a horse due to those powdermarks on his . . ."

"Yes, yes," interrupted the singed one, testily. "Get on with it. What is your idea, emptyhead?"

"Well," smiled Big Baby, "let us put the storekeeper on your horse, Heovese. Then I myself will carry you home all the way in my strong arms, and I will not once let the saddlehorn strike you in your poor powderburned . . ."

"Enough, enough!" winced the well-smoked Ute. "Listen, you're not so crazy, at that Maxemesevoto. My bottom is tender as a chapped baby's. Ai!ai! All right, we'll do it. Get that cursed white man down from there. Hurry. Careful, though, don't let the dog at him."

Big Baby grinned and led Yellow Nose's pony over toward the flagpole. He sighted up at Milch dangling above. He eyed Lame Wolf leaping at the base. "Just right," he announced aloud. And, whipping out his skinning knife, he slashed the halyards clean.

Milch rocketed straight down the pole, head-first. The dog never knew what hit him. The two skulls, that of man and that of man's best friend, came together with a crack like that of a splitting pine. Lame Wolf gave a great yelp and began to rush around screeching like he had been run over by a prairie schooner. Henry Milch, his plummeting fall broken by the dog's thick-furred body, staggered up in time for Big Baby to take him beneath the arms and lift him up and jam him down astride of Yellow Nose's stolen U.S. Cavalry saddle, and away went the Smoky Hill peace mission, spurring hard for home.

As for Lame Wolf, his head quit ringing after a bit and he commenced getting angry. He was more than angry; he was ashamed, humbled, made a fool of. Well, there had been two of those white men when he first took the trail from the store. Where was the other one hiding? He could not have gotten far. Things had happened much too swiftly for that. Let an old Cheyenne dog see now. Beginning at the iron pole, he would start quartering out in widening circles sniffing constantly to ground until—aha! there it was, as plain as the pad-scent of a she-wolf in the mating moon. Leading not to the gate, but veering away toward that building with the lamplight shining from it. Now, then, let them see if they could drop another white man on Lame Wolf's head. Let them just try it. This time it was for blood. White man's blood. Pony soldier blood. *Yi-yi-yi-yi-yi!* Away went the hairy brute racing through the night, nose glued to the scent of Cumpston Funder, mind fastened like trapjaws to the thought of not permitting *this* white man to get away.

**42**

THE NIGHT had grown oddly still when Funder reached
the infirmary. Behind him, he no longer heard the treeing
bays of Lame Wolf. Off to his left, over the parade ground
toward the store, he did think he heard Preacher Bleek's
memorable tones geeing and hawing his mules, and wondered, from that, if the Horse Creek giant were readying
to make his dash out of the fort. No matter, Funder had
headed him. In but moments, now, he would have the
stout lads out of their hospital cots and manning the main
gate. Moreover, among the night sounds made evident by
the strange hiatus of quiet, was one close at hand and
most intriguing.

Halting near the infirmary window, Funder bent his
ear.

Yes, it was coming from Major Hummerbund's surgery.
A late case? Some emergency sent over from the brawl at
Milch's store? A postoperative relapse of one of Bleek's
earlier victims from that morning's fight?

*Ting, ting, ting, ting.* What an oddly familiar, yet alien,
noise. If one didn't know better, he might think Hummerbund was in his cups again, and pitching buckshot into a
tin bucket for bets with the boys in the ward.

Funder could not resist the temptation to peek into the

surgery window, where a curl of the old window shade gave a good view of the table.

Sure enough, the good doctor was operating.

But not on a soldier.

On that gleaming table of white lay a large and strangely pale Cheyenne warrior, face down, rump up. And what Surgeon Hummerbund was plucking from the proffered stern were precisely what Funder's ears had imagined—buckshot! And the ringing noise came from the tin coffee cup held by Corporal Blemmish, Edward A., who stood anxiously beside the table counting aloud as each *ting* of recovered shot pellet struck the tin vessel in his trembling hand. With a start, Funder recognized the wounded Indian as Sergeant Stanley Schmerd.

"Thirty-eight, thirty-nine, forty, forty-one . . ."

"You see, Corporal," Funder could hear Hummerbund's muffled voice explaining, "the importance of the count is that, as an old crack-shot hunter of upland birds, I know exactly how many shot of whatever size are placed in each shell. If we come out with the correct, or total, number, then we know our friend Stanley won't be so apt to develop blood poisoning or lockjaw or gangrene, although the latter eventuality, at least the military gas variety, is always a distinct possibility in battlefield wounds."

Funder drew back from the window.

What luck. Tough old Sergeant Schmerd and blindly obedient Corporal Blemmish to aid in the main gate defense. A man's pot indeed sometimes ran over. No cavalry lieutenant felt truly armed without an old sergeant at his side. Now Funder had Schmerd. The rose was dew-pearled, the lark on the wing, all would yet be right with the western Kansas world.

But when the young officer burst into the infirmary

with his stirring alarum to man the stockades, he found something less than purblind fealty.

To begin with, the men in the sick ward, an annex to the surgery office, overheard the trumpet call to combat and when Funder shortly strode to their carbolic-tainted boudoir, he found only an open window, its curtains furling in the prairie breeze. The eight lively walking–wounded had flown as straightaway and out of range as any upland gamebird of Dr. Hummerbund's experience.

Well, there was still tough old Sergeant Stanley Schmerd and faithful Blemmish. Even inebriated Major Hummerbund might be brought to bear a musket in the breach. With himself, Funder, that made four. Concord had been won with seven. Thermopylae with three.

"Men!" he began, leaping back into the operating room. "Tonight, military history is ours! We four will make the stand that saved Fort Larking from its certain fall. We . . ."

Whatever else of courage and cavalry legend the lieutenant would have built was suspended in mid-gasp as a more compelling voice than his interrupted from without.

*Yi-yi-yi-yi-yi! Yi-yi-yi——*

Funder flashed to the infirmary window, shaded his eye, squinted into the outer moonglare.

As instantly, he flashed back from the window, his face sicklied o'er with incontinent cowardice.

"It's the wolf dog!" he cried. "Running my track. You must save me! You don't know that monster. He's a killer."

"Yes sir," said Blemmish, saluting. "That he is, sir."

As if in confirmation of the corporal's agreement, Lame Wolf arrived at the infirmary door. He hurled himself against its panels, leaped up to try and reach its transom ripped at its threshold crack with flailing forepaws in a mad effort to dig under it. Then, these things failing, he came for the window, a far frailer thing, his hoarse howl growing wilder all the while.

"Well, for the love of God!" shrieked Funder. "Don't just look at me, men. Fall in! Forward ho! HHhhellPP!"

"What can we do, sir?" asked Blemmish, with soldierly sincerity. "I ain't got no more innards than a cleaned chicken, sir."

"Yes," said Surgeon-Major Hummerbund, "and I am as drunk as a spotted skunk, and nowhere near so hostile."

"Don't look at me, Lieutenant!" warned Stanley Schmerd, reared on his elbow above the operating table. "I'm dying for the second time tonight." And with the dire croak, big Stanley rolled over and expired.

*Crrasshhh!*

The window glass shattered inward, showering the surgery with its shards.

"Compound fracture of the main pane," guessed Hummerbund, observing the splinterlines of the massive break. Then, nodding to the ball of hairy fury struggling upon the infirmary floor—which was Lame Wolf momentarily tangled in the window's sashcords and pulleyweights—he added a personal opinion to the professional estimate. "I should say, Cumpston, that you ought to be somewhere else when this animal frees himself, what?"

For a moment, Lieutenant Funder believed the end had come. Where might he run, that this terrible brute would not pursue and destroy him? Deserted by the ward soldiers, abandoned to his fate by the post surgeon, corporal *and* sergeant-of-the-guard, having in his own turn left to an unmentionable fate his commanding officer, having, in the final analysis, come down to the termination of the trail a man bereft alike of friend and fortune, there remained nothing for Cumpston Funder, Second Lieuten-

208

ant, United States Cavalry, to do save prepare to die like an officer and a gentleman.

"May I borrow your pistol, sir?" he asked, firm-lipped, of Major Hummerbund.

"No, no!" said Hummerbund. "You're not going to shoot that dog in my surgery!"

"It is not for the dog, sir, that I require the weapon," replied Funder, drawing himself erect. "By your leave, Major." He reached for Hummerbund's service revolver but the surgeon proved not so much the dog-lover as the neat housekeeper. He stepped beyond the lieutenant's grasp, pointing to the scrub sink on the farther wall.

"See here, man," he said indignantly, "if you've anything like that in mind, at least stand over the basin!"

There was no time to demur.

On the floor, Lame Wolf was twisting and foaming free of the last sashcord and pulleyweight.

Yet, just as Funder accepted the condition, moving toward the wall sink, Mars, the red god of the horse soldier, intervened. Clearly through the demolished window came the grizzly bear's bellow of Preacher Nehemiah Bleek urging on to greater flight toward main gate the lumbering Samson and the trim Delilah and the lathered Kiowa Ladies. In the same heaven-sent instant, the lieutenant saw, rocking past the infirmary in the stark light of the moon, the gaunt-ribbed white canvas top of the Argonaut. "Thank God!" he cried. "Salvation!" And, with the cry, dove headfirst and bullseye-center out through the gaping windowframe.

It was but half a snarl later that Lame Wolf gained his feet and lunged out the window after him. But Funder had the start. And he had, also, the angle on the nearing Argonaut. With a burst of speed which stripped from his flying limbs the very last of the pink taffeta ballgown, leaving the lieutenant in the same bareshanked state he had been when first forgotten atop the Argonaut by the little Arapaho girl Sunflower, at the time of the mule feeding, Funder made it to the highballing freight wagon with half-a-fang to spare ahead of the chopping jaws of Lame Wolf.

The clawing scramble of his ascent to the wagon's top, however, with the yowling unhappiness of the wolf dog at missing him again, brought the small round head of Sunflower popping out of the freighter's rear puckerhole.

Craning upward, her big brown eyes found Funder's bony white shins clamping the ribbed canvas above her.

"Oh!" she exclaimed apologetically. "Are you still up there, kind young one-bar pony soldier chief? I forgot all about you, didn't I? Come on down here into the wagon with the rest of us. It's all right, now, see—your dear friend Sunflower is here again to help you. Reach your hand to mine. That's it. Thank you."

Unstrung with gratitude, Funder slid limply in through the puckerhole and collapsed.

For him, as for the cheated Lame Wolf, the war was over, won by an eight-year-old Indian girl.

Oh, yes.

And by a two-hundred-and-forty-pound freelance preacher from Horse Creek, the Washita, Bent's Ranch and points West.

THE SMOKY HILL people have a saying that a truly good story, like a good moccasin or hunting shirt, stitches together all-swiftly in each of its many parts at the ending. If this be fair judgment, as well, for tales concerning white men, then perhaps a similar minstrel's blessing might attend the closing of the western Kansas legend of Nehemiah Bleek and The Day Fort Larking Fell.

Surely the sewing-up was swift.

If the fitting of the parts was not so precise, nor neat, it still must be said that what Preacher Bleek's blunt awl had brought together, stayed put. Neither in design nor needlework did the fabric of his defiance of the Federal Government fail, or fall apart.

The last the minions of that vaunted power—some of Strinker's men stumbling from post store to gaping main gate—saw of Preacher and his orphans of the Arkansas and Washita was the rear-end puckerhole of the Argonaut disappearing into the prairie moonlight toward the Smoky Hill, the small face of Sunflower beaming at them from afar and waving, with her child's clear cry from the tailgate, "Goodbye, goodbye, dear pony soldiers; see now my brother Little Chief salutes you in farewell—!" Which, indeed, Little Chief did. And was challenged at once by an indignant yowl from Lame Wolf, loping beneath the tailgate on his fastening-chain. All the Indian children leaned out the puckerhole—all of them from Horse Creek —and laughed at the old dog, who took it in good part and shook his head and galloped on, tongue lolling in a wolf's grin which split his wide and wicked face from battletorn ear to battletorn ear.

Lame Wolf knew the smell in that north wind stirring down from Smoky Hill. They were going home. Home to Indian country. Yi-yi-yi-yi! Who could be angry, even with Little Chief, the leaky small brother of Sunflower?

Within the warm body of the swaying freighter, the Horse Creek children took up the glad yelps of their hairy pet. The Washita children looked at them and, for the first time since the shrill dread of cavalry trumpets knifed the winter lodgeskins of their vanished band, laughed out loud. In the instant they too were yelping at Lame Wolf. Suddenly, there was hope in the old wagon. Young hearts had decided to beat again. Young eyes to look beyond the silent wastes of Stone Calf's camp. Good Preacher Bleek was taking them to new homes. Soon they would be with their own people once again. It was good to be in that old wagon. To have friends like Red Dust and Buzzard and Blackbird and Santiago by one's side in the darkness. Even the girl Sunflower was all right. *Ih-hai*, even her little brother, *he* might be worse. Not wetter, of course. Just worse.

And "The Cannonball," what of her?

That great warm friendly and yet dangerous ball of fat? Well, time would tell. She had shot that pony soldier sergeant on the wing, and very well. She had locked those other two soldiers in the small house out behind. She had taken the dog collar and the leash-rope off of Red Dust. And clearly she could fight. If adopted by the tribe, she

212

might indeed become the first female warrior in the history of the Cheyenne People. *Nohetto!* Give her a chance.

But what of the young one-bar pony soldier chief? He who sat crouched in the far corner of the wagon's bed, as he had from first tumbling-in. What of him? Was he a friend or foe? How were they to think of him, and he of them?

Sunflower settled that.

"He is my friend," she told the other children, putting one chubby arm through Funder's bony one, and snuggling to the wordless lieutenant. "He is kind to mules and plays very nice with the dog." She turned the huge brown eyes upward. "If the Washita children do not want you," she told him, "you can join our Horse Creek family. We can always use a good mule feeder."

All of the Horse Creek foundlings clapped hands and grinned in agreement to this.

"*Wagh!*" cried Blackbird. "*Vahé, veho!*"

"What did he say?" whispered Funder to Sunflower.

"He said '*wagh*,' the courage-word, and then he said, 'Welcome, white man,'" the Arapaho girl replied. "That's pretty generous of him when you think that Blackbird is one-half buffalo soldier."

It was more than just generous, Funder knew. Glancing at Blackbird and the other children, he lowered his eyes.

These wild dark-skinned sons and daughters of the prairie, whole or mixed of breed, their entire brief lives spent in flight from white emigrant, settler, cavalry soldier, had just accepted him. Funder, who had never had one friend, suddenly had the offer of many.

The young lieutenant, a misfit and a failure in his own world, could not grasp entirely the reality of the proposal that he might so easily be a success in this other, simpler life now tendered him by the red waifs of Horse Creek and the Washita. But one facet of the invitation shone clearly before him, and he leaped to the tailgate, pale face inspired, to wave and shout back, even as Sunflower before him, his glad farewell to Fort Larking and the U.S. Cavalry.

Then, the past sundered, he returned to the Indian children. Heart at rest and head held high in the first real dignity he had ever known, Cumpston Funder touched the fingertips of his left hand to his brow, in the Cheyenne manner. "Thank you, Blackbird," was all he said. *"Wagh!"*

The wild children of the Washita laughed happily at the strange sound of their tongue in the mouth of the skinny young pony soldier. Then, in that same tongue Red Dust, peering about in the wagon's gloom, asked with good spirit, "Now where is the fat one, Old Cannonball? Don't you think we should make her formal welcome, also? Ought we not bring her great bulk into the tipi-circle, as well? I think so, surely. Else it would be unkind and she will feel lonesome."

"Ha!" puffed Good Feather, the Washita girl. "She may feel lonesome but that is not what Preacher is feeling!"

Red Dust followed the pointing of her slim finger.

"Damn to hell!" admitted the nephew of Roman Nose, lapsing into the fractured English of the educated Indian. "You right like Lord Jesus. Look him front seat of wagon!"

As one the dusky children stared.

There beyond the forward puckerhole, haunch to bear-like haunch upon the pitch and sway of the driver's box, sat Preacher Nehemiah Bleek and Wee Katie Mehaffey. Overhead sailed the prairie's Big Frost Moon. Under-wheel bent the velvet rustle of the winter-curing buffalo grass. Out front, old evil Samson, spotted Delilah, and the lip-curled Kiowa Ladies were running light and yeasty as yearling broomtail colts, the winds of home within their belling nostrils, the lift of freedom to their flying heels.

But on the rocking seat of the ancient freighter, hearts soared higher and hands clasped tighter than winter moons or wagon mules or Indian mustang mares might ever again inspire.

As Kate had said so long ago to Captain Julius Caesar Strinker; " 'Tis love, yez blithering idjut—!"

And so indeed it was.

WILL HENRY was born and reared in Missouri, and attended college in Kansas City. In the quarter-century since leaving school he has lived in the far west. Working as ranchhand, gold miner, small-town newspaperman, he has learned of the land and its people by first-hand experience. He began to write his books in 1950, convinced that our frontier past deserved more truthful telling than it had been given in most so-called western stories. His books have reflected this feeling. Will Henry characters speak the truth, whether of cowboy, Indian, cavalryman, cattle rustler, prospector, outlaw, settler, sheepherder, or sheriff. Mr. Henry does not believe in writing down for the young person. Such past works as *Maheo's Children, In the Land of the Mandans, Sons of the Western Frontier,* and *Custer's Last Stand* colorfully demonstrate his faith in the intellectual hunger and understanding of the young reader.

Will Henry presently lives in California, where he devotes full time to the researching and writing of his books based in American history. His faith is in the land, Mr. Henry says, and in the youth of the land.